'Don't you think you owe me an explanation, Dixie?'

She didn't answer.

'You walked out on me seven years ago without even a word!' Connar rammed his hands deep into his pockets.

'I left a note.'

The anger was there in his face and his voice. *'I think it's better if I leave now. It will never work.* That's what you wrote. What the hell was I supposed to do, Dixie?'

Dear Reader

The nights are drawing in again... the perfect excuse for snuggling up with a Mills & Boon romance! November is the time for bonfires and fireworks, of course— and you'll find plenty of sparks flying between the heroes and heroines in this month's collection of love stories! Look out for books by some of you favourite authors... and if you're missing the summer sun, why not let us transport you to sunny California and exotic Mexico? So shut out the winter darkness, and enter the warm and wonderful world of Mills & Boon!

The Editor

Vanessa Grant began writing her first romance when she was twelve years old, The novel foundered on page fifty, but Vanessa never forgot the magic of having a love-story come to life. Although she went on to become an accountant and a college instructor, she never stopped writing, and in 1985 her first Mills & Boon novel was published. Vanessa and her husband live in a log home in the forest on one of British Columbia's Gulf Islands.

Recent titles by the same author:

YESTERDAY'S VOWS

BY
VANESSA GRANT

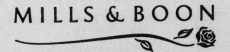

MILLS & BOON

MILLS & BOON LIMITED
ETON HOUSE, 18-24 PARADISE ROAD
RICHMOND, SURREY TW9 1SR

for Cameron and Faith—
have a wonderful life together

*MILLS & BOON and the Rose Device
are trademarks of the publisher.*

*First published in Great Britain 1994
by Mills & Boon Limited*

© Vanessa Grant 1994

*Australian copyright 1994 Philippine copyright 1994
This edition 1994*

ISBN 0 263 78463 0

*Set in Times Roman 10½ on 12 pt
01-9411-50240 C*

Made and printed in Great Britain

CHAPTER ONE

EIGHT hours was too long. She should have walked right up to Connar and faced him this morning at the exhibition. 'Let's talk,' she should have said. Then they could have spoken every word that needed saying between them over a shiny cafeteria table with the safety of people all around. Instead Dixie had spent the day dreading this meeting, and she felt no more prepared for it now than she had in that first instant of seeing him earlier today.

At first she had intended to arrive early, to be there at the end of Shelter Island waiting when he came. She'd meant to drive her van there, to park in the car park and climb out on the rocks where she could wait for him with the ocean at her back.

Only then she'd started to think of all the things that might go wrong, like Connar taking her licence plate number as she left and using it to find her again. She had Mexican Baja plates. If he knew to look in Mexico...

Connar coming to her door. Jess answering.

She knew she was paranoid. He probably didn't give a damn where she lived. Seven years, and she was a loose end in his life, that was all. It was just bad luck that he'd wandered into that San Diego mall earlier today—that he'd stopped at the gallery and seen her pictures. He must have recognised her name on a portrait, and he wanted to see her because he could hardly just walk away. Connar always hated loose ends. Other than that there was no reason for him to care about the details of her life.

She didn't know if she believed that or not, but she didn't drive the van out to Shelter Island. She took a taxi instead, and she was late. She shivered as the taxi driver turned on to the road that led out the Shelter Island causeway. This was a weekend place, a nature walk for city people. It wasn't a real island, because you could drive to it along the narrow causeway where green grass and park benches stretched into the harbour. It was a beautiful place to walk with a lover, or even alone. When she'd come here other times there had been a reassuring number of people around, and that was what she'd pictured when she'd chosen this place to meet Connar. But now in the early evening there was hardly anyone in sight.

She should have arranged to meet him somewhere there were crowds. The middle of the mall would have been ideal. They could talk. She could leave, and he'd never know any more than he did this minute. He could ask Ernie, but Ernie wasn't going to tell secrets he didn't know, so if Dixie didn't tell ...

Connar had been like a big brother when she was little, always taking over and taking charge of her life when he thought she'd messed up. She was twenty-seven now, too old for looking after, but he might not see that. He might not be at all willing to simply say, 'How are you?' and 'Goodbye'. He might insist on knowing more, on seeing every detail of her life. And he'd always had a knack for finding out the things she wanted hidden. The year she was eleven he'd found her hiding-place in the old cabin by the beach. On her fifteenth birthday she'd run away, and it was Connar who had found her, Connar who had persuaded her home with logic and charm.

This morning she had been only a hundred feet from his broad back when someone had moved and she'd seen him. She'd been frozen by his image for a second, exactly the way it happened when she passed a television in a store display with Connar's image watching her from the screen. Then her brain kicked in with the knowledge that this wasn't an image. This was Connar, real and alive, and if he turned he would see her!

She had run then, breathing hard, and panicked until she knew he hadn't followed. But he had her scent now. She knew she had to face him, to settle whatever needed settling between them. So she'd telephoned the gallery, standing in an outside phone booth dressed in shorts and a T-shirt, with Connar vivid in her memory.

A truck had roared past just as Ernie answered the gallery telephone. 'Ernie,' she'd hissed, 'don't say my name! It's Dixie.'

'Where the devil are you? Got a customer here. You'll never guess who——'

She'd gulped. 'I know who he is.'

How did he think of her? As the child who had tagged after him? As a difficult adolescent who had avoided skirts like a plague? Or dressed in plain black and crying the day of her father's funeral?

. . . Or naked in his arms, begging him to love her?

Ernie's excitement had come distorted over the telephone. 'That fellow on the news? The one they call indestructible? He wants to buy the *Cat Girl* original.'

Indestructible.

She had stopped watching television news for almost a year when they started calling him the indestructible Stanford, talking about how he always turned up, how he'd disappeared in the war-torn Middle East...in the racial violence of South Africa. He had been reported as kidnapped and missing and presumed dead at different times over the years. But he always turned up in the end, they said. And when he did he had the inside story that no one else had dared go after. She'd been terrified when she heard that, haunted, because she knew he wouldn't stop taking chances until the day he lost everything.

'It's not for sale,' she had told Ernie. She had fought a wave of dizziness. It was an accident that it was Jess's picture. Any picture would have done. Connar would be asking after the original as a device to get close to Dixie, close enough to get hold of her and bawl her out, the way he had all those years ago when she had gone swimming despite Aunt Jessie's orders. 'The *Cat Girl* original isn't for sale,' she'd repeated. Her voice had felt brittle.

'Dixie, anything's for sale if the customer is willing to pay enough. The thing is, he wants to meet you. He's just gone off to... There he is, coming back now. How long will you be?'

Dixie had watched enough television news to know that Connar Stanford would go to any lengths to get the story. If she ran now he'd pursue with the same instinct that sent a dog pounding after a panicked house cat.

'Dixie?'

'Is he there?'

'Yeah. What happened to you, anyway? You——'

'Tell him . . .' She had squeezed her eyes closed and whispered, 'Tell him I'll meet him tonight at seven.'

'What the hell? Dixie, I close at six.'

'On Shelter Island,' she'd hissed. 'Out at the far end.'

So here she was, on her way to meet Connar, and she knew it was a terrible idea meeting him here . . . meeting him at all.

She saw him as the taxi driver turned into the car park at the end of the island. The park served the harbour police building and the docks where visiting yachts berthed. She saw grass and the rocky man-made shoreline and Connar standing near the shore with his back to her, as if he was staring out towards the harbour entrance and the sun that would set soon. His shoulders; that impatient flex of muscles. She'd seen that motion often enough—Connar pretending to stand patiently while everything inside him was racing towards the future, his mind on some distant and violent part of the world.

He turned as the taxi stopped. Her hands trembled as she paid the taxi driver. Connar wasn't close enough for her to see the frown pulling his eyebrows down, but she knew it was there. She slung her handbag strap over her shoulder and slammed the door of the taxi closed. Then she stood erect and stared across the roof of the taxi at Connar. All she could see was his face as he moved closer, his eyes holding hers until he was

close enough that she could see she hadn't exag-
gerated the depth of their blue magnetism.

'I thought you weren't coming,' he said when he
stopped walking.

The taxi reversed, leaving nothing between them
except eight feet of pavement and almost seven years
of time. She pushed her handbag strap higher on her
shoulder. He was wearing a pale blue short-sleeved
shirt that echoed the darker blue of his eyes. The shirt
was open at the neck, exposing the beginning of the
tangled blond curls of his chest hair.

The wind from the sea twisted around her and
moulded her skirt against her legs. She'd dressed for
him, in a drifting cotton skirt in a colour that echoed
the way her hair moved from brown to red in different lights. Once she'd thought he liked her hair,
his eyes tangling in the long curls she had used to wear.
The hair was short now, but she'd worn the skirt and
a matching blouse embroidered in an intricate Mexican
pattern. He'd seen her mostly in jeans and shorts, and
she wanted to show him that she had changed, that
she was no child in need of his protection. She hadn't
realised as she dressed that she'd also wanted his eyes
to flash with the hot emotion she'd once lured there.

No emotion in his eyes now. Just cold blue staring
at her, and his mouth frowning. She wished she could
clear her throat without giving away the tension
crawling in her.

'I thought about not coming,' she admitted in a
husky voice.

She had driven south across the Mexican border
after that phone call to Ernie. She'd felt relief as she
drove through the border, as if the international

boundary were a gate that closed off Connar's access to her. On Mexican soil she'd driven too fast and promised herself that there was no need to come back, no need to meet Connar. Except that she had sent him a message to say that she would meet him.

It wouldn't have been the first promise broken between them.

'What changed your mind?' he asked now.

She made her shoulders move in a shrug. Seven years, and she was no young girl to be intimidated by Connar's agenda. On her television she had watched powerful men lose secrets under Connar's questioning. She had to be stronger than those men.

'Knowing you,' she said, 'I figured if you wanted to talk to me you'd hang around until you got what you wanted.'

'I've got a car.' He gestured towards the car park. 'Let's go somewhere.'

She had to fight the old pull of his magnetism. The last article Dixie had read about him had described Connar Stanford as 'irresistibly sexy'. The tamed wildness of dark blond waves. The lean, graceful strength of a virile man. The woman who'd written that article had probably tried to make Connar want her. Dixie had stared at the words and wondered painfully whether Conn had taken time to enjoy the reporter's charms.

He might have. If so, in the end he'd have left her. Connar Stanford would be on the front wave of the world until the day it killed him. What woman could compete with that?

She cleared her throat. 'We can talk here.' She buried her hands in the deep pockets of her skirt. 'There can't be much to say.'

Once he would have let the anger show. She saw that he was less impulsive now. Emotion flashed into his eyes, but nothing showed in his face, and his voice was soft when it came.

'Are you afraid to get into a car with me?'

She lifted her chin. 'When I was ten years old you got me up on that diving-board with a taunt like that. A dare. Not now.'

He stepped closer, and she tensed to stop herself jumping back.

'Dixie, just what do you imagine I'll do to you if you get into my car?'

She shrugged with what she hoped looked like indifference.

'Do you think I'll try to make love to you?'

She felt the heat crawl up her throat, remembering Connar coming through the door into his room, the room where he'd slept all those years—but that last time she had been waiting for him. She recalled Connar staring at her and the sick sudden realisation that he hadn't intended her to be here. Then it had been too late and he had been touching her, consuming her sanity with the passion that drove her restless and heated in dreams.

'You'll try to take control.' She stripped her voice of feeling. 'It's what you do, isn't it? Take control. You don't ask what anyone else wants. You just——'

'It wasn't me doing the asking that night,' he snapped. 'You were the one who issued the invitation.

And that leaves us with a few things to talk about.'
If she hadn't seen the anger in his eyes she would have
believed the boredom reflected in his voice.

'I'm not going anywhere, Connar.' She stood with
her legs parted slightly, and felt her fingers curling
into fists. 'Not with you.'

'I didn't know you hated me.'

She turned away before her throat could form an
answer. Off the point of the land a sailboat was racing
past, flying a large, brilliantly striped spinnaker. She
moved across the grass towards the rocks of the shore,
as if she could reach the racing yacht and escape his
probing voice.

'When did you cut your hair, Dix?'

She looked and he was only a step behind, one hand
still buried casually in his pocket, the other swinging
free. The blue shirt was creased where he'd tucked it
into the waist of his trousers, then pulled tightly as it
rose towards the breadth of his chest. She stared at
the place where she knew a curve of muscle flexed
when he moved his arm. She remembered her own
hand curved there, remembered the play of strength
in him as he had moved over her.

She clutched the strap of her purse and held on
tightly, afraid some madness might cause her hand to
reach for his, seeking old dreams . . . impossible
dreams.

'I've never seen it short before,' he said.

'I—I cut it seven years ago.' He was too close. The
danger was here and now, not back in her history. She
turned abruptly and stepped on to the rocks.

'Watch your step!'

When she balanced on the rock and turned back to
see him, he seemed a confusing mixture of the reporter
on her television and the young Connar she'd
worshipped a long time ago. She knew every line of
his face, had memorised the way his eyes narrowed
when he grinned, the way the lines cut into his cheeks
when he frowned. She knew the frowns better than
the smiles, because of the places he'd been since she
left him. She was used to seeing him with broken
buildings behind him . . . starving children . . . riots.

Not standing right here, watching her.

'I won't fall,' she said.

'You've told me that before.'

'I was a child then.' He was reaching out, his hand
stretching towards her, the muscles flexing on his
forearm. She sucked in an unsteady breath. 'I'm not
a child now.'

'You look about twelve. Why did you cut your
hair?'

'It was in the way,' she said raggedly.

Every time she'd brushed it she had remembered.
She had been staring up at him, her hair spread all
around her on the bed. His eyes had been dark and
shadowed, watching her. His fingers had tangled in
the streaming waves, and his voice had been husky
with passion and surprise.

'Conn. . .' She cleared the memories from her throat.
'What is it you want, Connar?'

He frowned, and she was glad she'd backed away
from him to this rock where she had safety of a sort.
It was a small rock, four feet away from where he
stood on the grass, with sharp sides and nothing
around, so that he'd have to take a big stride to get

here, and there was no room except the place where she stood. He couldn't reach out and touch her, couldn't press close unless he wanted to take a chance on making her fall.

'What do you think I'd want?'

She shrugged and pressed her lips together. She had a clear memory of a much younger Connar talking about techniques, about making the other person talk first and learning a lot that way. She stared at him, but his eyes had turned so dark that they were more black than blue, emotion concealed in darkness. Behind him she could see a police car slowly cruising through the car park.

He lifted his head as if he'd sensed something from her expression. 'Don't you think you owe me an explanation, Dixie?'

She didn't answer.

'You walked out on me seven years ago without even a word!' He rammed his hands deep into his pockets. 'We can't settle that with two minutes' talk on the edge of the ocean.'

'I left a note.' Standing on this rock was a mistake. She had nowhere to go. 'I left a note,' she repeated.

'That you did.' His eyes had narrowed, and the lines cut deep around his mouth. She'd thought the anger was locked under control, but it was there in his face and his voice. '"I think it's better if I leave now. It will never work!". That's what you wrote. What the hell was I supposed to do, Dixie?'

She pushed her hands into the pockets of the skirt and hunched her shoulders. 'File the note. Go catch your plane. That's what you were doing anyway.' She felt the need to move restlessly, and fought it. 'What

difference did it make where I was? What difference
can it possibly make now?' This was terrible. Connar
staring at her, and she didn't know what he was
thinking, except that he was angry. Maybe she'd never
understood what he was thinking.

He held out his hand towards her. 'Come off that
rock. We can't talk like this.'

'We've nothing to talk about.'

'You're still my wife.' The words died on the wind.
Behind Connar the police car lurched into motion,
lights flashing as it screamed round in a circle and
headed down the causeway. Behind her the sailboat
must still be flying before the wind.

'But didn't . . .?' She gulped. 'I thought you'd have
divorced me.'

His hand was still extended towards her. Unwillingly she let her hand join his, and he pulled her
towards the grass. Towards him. 'Have you had
dinner?' he demanded. His mouth was a straight line,
eyes narrowed. Two feet between them, and her hand
still caught in his.

'No.' She felt as if she were trapped in a time warp,
Connar leading her by the hand, pulling her towards
his car. It had been like that when he had come to
take her out of art college. She'd been twenty, alone
in the world except for Connar, who had come to take
over her life. She jerked to a halt two steps before
they got to the compact car. She pulled on her hand,
but he wouldn't release it.

'What is it you want from me?'

'A better atmosphere for our conversation,'
he muttered.

She jerked her hand, and this time he let it free. 'And what else?'

'Answers. Why did you run? Where are you living?'

She smoothed her hands along the folds of her cotton skirt. 'You've had eight hours to check up on me and you haven't been able to find out a little thing like where I live?'

His eyes were narrowed, studying her as if she were a specimen under a microscope. 'If you weren't deliberately hiding, I'd have found you years ago. Why did you run away?'

She remembered the morning she had left, remembered the look on his face and the moment when she'd understood everything. 'I just—it was a mistake. Getting married.'

'A mistake?' His voice was neutral, and he stood waiting for her to explain. She tried to fight the urge to let words babble into the silence. Failed.

'I realised . . . I knew if I'd tried to tell you . . . you wouldn't have let me go. So I . . .' She spread her hands. 'I simply left. What does it matter now?'

He turned and jerked the car door open. He gestured for her to get in.

She sucked in a shaky breath. 'You haven't changed at all. I'm not getting in that car. I'm sorry you've been—*inconvenienced* by my disappearing, but you're not taking over my life again.' She gestured vaguely towards the road. 'Go back to wherever you're spending your time these days, but first take the time to call your lawyer. Divorce me. You should have done it years ago.'

His hands tightened on the car door. She stepped back, suddenly afraid he might force her into his car.

'If only you hadn't happened to see those pictures today,' she whispered.

Suddenly the angles of his face seemed harsher. 'I found you a week ago. Your picture's on a publicity piece on the back of one of your prints. It was hanging in the network chief's office in New York.'

A week. She'd been driving back and forth across the border. She'd even brought Jess up to the States twice. It was only luck that she hadn't had Jess with her today. Jess had wanted to go to the beach with Sue, and at the last minute plans had been changed.

Some day he would have to know about Jess. But not today!

'I see you on television,' she whispered. He was staring at her, and the words just crept out. She flushed and stared down at her sandals. 'On the news, but not much lately. Where have you——?'

'You never had the urge to look me up?'

She gulped. 'I told you I wasn't coming back. In the note.'

'For all I knew you were dead.'

She lifted her head. 'You could have been dead a thousand times by now.' His hand reached towards her, and she jerked away. 'I couldn't *bear* the thought of spending my life dreading it happening again, seeing it on television...' Her voice rose, and she couldn't stop it. '*Watching* as if it were just the evening news, and seeing... I'll never forget seeing my father hit by that terrorist bullet. And you—damn you, Connar! Get out of my life!'

The colour had left his face. 'You saw Dev get hit?' His eyes turned black. 'Why didn't you tell me you saw that?'

She wrapped her arms around her waist. 'What difference does it make?'

He crossed the four feet of pavement between them. She backed away from him, but it was too late. He was there, in front of her, towering over her, and she was breathing in the scent and the feel of him. His hands fastened on her arms, and she felt herself moving closer instead of pulling back, aware of the swirl of hair on the backs of his forearms, his fingers curled into her shoulders.

'It doesn't make sense,' he muttered, and she could feel the words resonating through his chest. Too close. She tried to pull away, a desperate jerk against his grip. 'I don't believe you,' he said. 'That's not why you ran.'

She shrugged, and the motion made his fingers dig into her shoulders. Her flesh crawled with response, as if he'd caressed her body with passion.

'You would have said something,' he insisted. 'When I asked you to marry me you'd have said. You knew my job and you knew the risks. You——'

'When you *asked* me?' She was trembling deep inside, but she stared into his eyes with her own angry gaze. With every breath she took she felt his fingers pressing on her flesh through the blouse as she muttered, 'You made the decision for me. "I think we should get married", you said. You married me because you believed I couldn't look after myself and, as you can see, you were wrong. You don't know me, Connar. I—— Get your hands off me before I scream! I don't *need* looking after! If you still feel obligated by that promise to my father, forget it. There's...' She swallowed, and pulled against his grip.

'My promise to Dev has nothing to do with this.'

She laughed then, and it sounded brittle to her own ears. 'But you pay your debts, don't you? And you owe a lot to Devlin Bradshaw. And—I...' She shivered at the emotion that flashed into his eyes. Jess looked at her just like that sometimes. When she was angry. When she wanted something Dixie wouldn't let her have.

She had to tell him about Jess. She knew she had to. But not now. Not today, with Connar's eyes blazing with angry determination. Not with his hands on her and her pulse echoing every flicker in his eyes.

'I want an explanation.' His voice was hard now, the way she'd sometimes heard it on television. 'Why did you run away?'

'I don't owe you an explanation.'

'I think you do.'

She caught her lip between her teeth, released it when his eyes narrowed. 'Why didn't you divorce me?' she asked on a whisper.

'I made a promise,' he said grimly.

She'd known for long enough how empty the marriage was, but it hurt that his promise to her father had meant more than the anger he must have felt towards her when she had run.

'Where are you living, Dixie?'

She drew in a ragged breath. 'I'm not inviting you into my home, so you've no need to know where I live.' If he knew about Jess he'd take over. He would take control and stuff Dixie into whatever he thought was her proper place in his life. She threw her head back and glared at him. 'Do you want a place to serve the divorce papers?'

'I want an explanation, Dixie, but yes—I want a divorce. I want to get on with my life.'

'You haven't exactly been wasting away the years.' She shook her hair back and wished for the long waves she'd cut off when she left Connar. Something to hide behind. 'Use Ernie's address for the papers,' she said. 'I'll give you his card. Let go of me, Connar.'

'You're still my wife.' His hands tightened on her shoulders.

'Your wife?' she mocked. 'Every word you said in that ceremony was a lie. And being your wife... These days that doesn't give you the right to manhandle me.'

He pulled her closer. She wanted to pull away, to scream. His eyes stopped her. She could feel the heat radiating from his body. His shoulders were broader than they had been seven years ago. More muscle, more hard strength. She felt her own body responding, breasts swelling as if his masculinity called to the softness in her.

He released her so abruptly that she staggered slightly.

'Give me the card, then,' he ground out. 'The address.'

An address for divorce papers. A separation between them, a legal disengagement. Afterwards... after it was over and he had no claim on her, she would tell him about Jess. However dangerous Connar Stanford was to her, she knew that one day she must tell him he had a daughter.

'Let me get this straight,' said Sue. She was sitting cross-legged on Dixie's bed in the little cottage just north of Ensenada, Mexico. She was watching Dixie.

fold the laundry. She extended the manicured fingers of one hand and frowned as she counted on each finger. 'First, this man is Jessica's father?'

Dixie dropped the jeans. They landed on the bed on top of a neatly folded pile of Jess's shorts and T-shirts. From the next room came the sound of young laughter—Jess playing with Maria, a neighbour child. There was one sharp excited bark from Wolf, their mongrel dog.

'Yes,' she said dully. 'I told you that—I told you a long time ago.' Dixie picked up the jeans and twisted her fingers in the denim fabric. Hardly anyone knew who Jess's father was. Just Sue, because six years ago Sue's offer had made it possible for Dixie to give her baby a home while she found a way to support both herself and her daughter.

And Jess knew, because last year Jess had asked and Dixie had shown her Connar on the television. One day soon Jess would ask more questions. Dixie kept expecting questions that hadn't come yet.

Sue shook back her long red hair and pointed out reasonably, 'You showed me a man on a television screen. You said he wasn't interested in anything but news from Timbuktu and the moon. But he's here now and he's obviously interested.' Sue stretched out her second finger. 'He says you're his wife. And you— you're hiding from him, won't talk to him, won't see him.' The older woman made a gesture that threw away the items she'd counted on her fingers. 'You're in love with the man and he's here on your door-step——'

'I'm *not* in love with him! It's just that he still...that he has this...this physiological effect on me. It certainly isn't *love*!' She bit her lip and stared down at the jumbled jeans. 'He'll find me, you know. He was angry when I drove off in that taxi.'

They'd been standing face to face in the car park when the taxi had driven up. Dixie had panicked and run towards the yellow taxi. The last she'd seen of Connar, he'd been watching her drive away with a look on his face that told her it wasn't over. 'He'll have taken the number of the cab,' she muttered. 'By now he'll know exactly where I went.'

Sue didn't believe it. 'You told me the taxi took you to the San Diego trolley. He can hardly find you from a trolley station! You're fantasising that you're a character in a spy story!'

'Connar has tracked down spies,' said Dixie dismally. She folded the jeans with an angry motion. 'He'll find me. He'll find out about Jess. And then…'

Sue slid off the bed and on to her feet. 'Give this whole thing a bit of thought, Dixie. You've been hung up on this guy for years. I've known you for six years, and in that time you haven't looked seriously at another man. And now he's come after you. Why not give the guy a chance?'

Dixie shook her head. 'You don't understand,' she whispered.

In the early days after she left him she'd expected to find him following her… knocking on the door of the room she'd rented to sleep in… touching her shoulder when she was on the bus. She had known the risk and had disappeared as completely as possible. Connar knew how to find people, but she had been determined that he wouldn't find *her*.

She'd been careful not to go anywhere he might guess. She'd cut herself off, hadn't written or phoned anyone. She'd done her banking in one transaction, had withdrawn all her money in cash and then fled fifteen hundred miles away from that bank. She'd known it was crazy, paranoid, but if Connar had found her back then . . .

She couldn't have handled it then.

She wasn't certain she could handle it now.

CHAPTER TWO

WHEN Dixie's father took her to live with Jessie
Stanford on Thetis Island, he made her two promises.
She remembered staring up at him as he spoke. She
had a long way to look up, because she was only six
years old.

He promised Dixie that she would be happy with
Mrs Stanford. 'And I'll come for you every year on
your birthday.' He gave her the smile that always made
her feel special as he promised, 'We'll go away for
our own holidays. Just you and me. Every year on
your birthday. I promise, honey.'

She believed him.

Devlin Bradshaw could hardly have done better than
to place his daughter in Jessie Stanford's care. Dixie
missed her mommy, but her mother was gone forever
in a car crash, and the woman she learned to call Aunt
Jessie was soft and loving. Her father was right—she
was happy living with the Stanfords.

Every year on her birthday, he promised, but there
were reasons why he couldn't keep that promise. He
would usually call on the telephone a few days before
her birthday. She would hold the receiver tightly
against her ear while he explained about a crisis in
Warsaw or an aircraft disaster in the Pacific. He
wanted to be with her, but important news
was breaking.

'Sorry, honey, but this thing came up in Berlin. I'll make it up to you next time. Watch me on the news and I'll give you our special smile. You understand, don't you?'

Dixie always said she understood.

Aunt Jessie would let Dixie stay up late to watch the news on the nights her father called. Devlin Bradshaw reported significant events. From infancy she had been told how important his work was. She treasured the smile that was his signal for her, the crooked tilt of his lips as he said, 'This is Devlin Bradshaw reporting...' From Berlin or Athens or Paris, he always smiled like that for her. It was a code between them, the smile that no one else knew was for his daughter on the west coast of Canada. She kept that smile a secret. She didn't even tell Connar.

Aunt Jessie's son Connar was thirteen when Dixie came to the Stanford farm. The day after Dixie arrived, scared and already missing her father terribly, Connar took her to the tree-house he'd built in a big maple in the woods.

'You can use it,' he offered. 'Whenever you like. It can be your secret place.'

Dixie thought she probably fell in love with Connar that day.

Her dad sent presents when he couldn't come. Occasionally he flew in unexpectedly and spent a few days at Jessie's farm, taking Dixie for walks that Connar tagged along on. Connar asked questions that made Devlin Bradshaw talk about things he never discussed with Dixie. She loved walking between the lanky teenage Connar and her tall father, loved listening to Connar's questions and her dad's magical accounts of the world through the eyes of a television news correspondent.

As Dixie grew up she came to understand that her father paid Jessie Stanford to make a home for his daughter. Jessie needed the money, bringing up Connar alone and working the marginal little farm sprawled along the shore of Thetis Island. But Jessie treated her as a daughter, and Dixie never felt like a paid boarder. She knew Aunt Jessie loved her.

Connar also treated Dixie as if she belonged to the family. He protected her and bawled her out when she got in trouble. He teased her into laughter when she was crying, and sometimes he talked to her about his own dreams.

Dixie was seven when she decided to marry Connar when she grew up. At her eighth birthday party she made the mistake of telling him about her decision. He was showing her how to roast marshmallows on a stick, and she had just dropped the third messy marshmallow into the fire. She cried and he gave her a casual hug. Then he shoved another marshmallow on to the stick for her.

'This one will work,' he said.

She smiled at him through her tears. 'You'll marry me when I grow up, won't you, Conn? That's what I want.'

He went very still. 'Watch the marshmallow. Hold the stick up...' He smiled then, but he stepped back from her as he said, 'You'll fall in love with someone else, Dix.'

'No, I won't,' she insisted.

'You'll have to, because I'm not going to be around. I'm going to be a news correspondent like your dad.'

She didn't ask again, but she held the dream close through the years. When she grew up she would be beautiful like her mother. Connar would fall in love with her, and they'd get married just as her mommy and daddy had. Dixie believed in dreams coming true. Her mommy had always told her that if she wished hard enough she could have anything she really wanted. So she wished and she planned, and she followed the rules about wishes and kept it secret.

Connar would grow up and became a correspondent. Dixie would grow up and marry him. They would live where the news was, in London and Athens and Paris. She would follow Connar wherever he went and she would never be left behind waiting for phone calls again.

The summer Dixie was nine she hardly saw Connar. He was spending all his time with Elsie Tarran, who had come to visit her grandparents. Elsie had been on the island at Easter, and back then Connar had agreed when Dixie said that Elsie was silly. She wore too much nail polish and she had a wild addiction to hairspray. But between Easter and July Connar changed his mind.

Dixie disliked Elsie, but obviously Conn didn't. She saw Conn and Elsie sitting together on the ferry to town with their hands tangled together... Conn and Elsie lying in the long grass by the beach...

That was the worst moment. On the beach. Dixie came running down to the beach from the house, tearing through the bushes and screaming to a stop, because she hadn't known anyone was there. And she didn't think too much about what she saw then. It was years later that the memory hurt.

She didn't understand when she saw Connar's mouth tangled with Elsie's and their bodies together the way she'd seen couples on television. Dixie didn't understand what they were doing, but she did know that Connar was slipping away from her.

When she was twelve he went away to university in Vancouver. She missed him with an ache that dulled with time but never left her entirely. Whenever he came home Dixie followed him everywhere. He worked on the farm during holidays, and Dixie helped. When she couldn't help she sat on fences, on stools in the barn—anywhere she could be near Connar. He talked and she listened, and when she told him that she was going to be an artist he didn't laugh.

He never laughed at her dreams. By the time her fifteenth birthday was approaching she was sophisticated enough to understand that there must be girls he went with at university, girls he touched as he had touched Elsie that summer in the tall grass. It didn't matter. One day she would be old enough. One day he would look at her the way he'd looked at Elsie. She grew up clutching that dream.

Her father called to promise he'd be there for her fifteenth birthday in December. They would go to Vancouver for a concert, then dinner and an overnight stay in a very luxurious hotel. During the last week before her birthday Dixie flew into the house breathlessly after school each day, demanding, 'Did anyone call?'

'Your dad hasn't called,' Aunt Jessie always answered. 'Don't worry. He'll be here. You'll have your birthday.'

Friday was her birthday, and he was coming on Thursday. When he didn't call by Wednesday night she knew it was going to be all right. But Thursday came and Devlin Bradshaw didn't. No telephone call. Nothing. She watched the news and her father wasn't there on television either. He'd forgotten, and she was devastated because somehow she'd believed that this time he would come. But he'd not come and he'd actually forgotten her, hadn't even called to cancel.

When Aunt Jessie tried to talk to her about it Dixie ran out of the house and into the woods, where she cried up in the tree-house until she was exhausted. He'd forgotten her completely.

A long time later she went into the house and sneaked into the office, where she dialled Connar's telephone number in Vancouver. If she could only talk to Conn she'd be all right. Conn would tell her that her father cared, that everything would be all right.

But Conn's room-mate answered and told her Connar was out with his girlfriend. Connar had always been there for her, and it hurt terribly that he was with another girl now when she needed him so badly. Connar and her father had both abandoned her.

Her father probably hadn't really wanted to come to her birthday in the first place. But he'd promised her a concert, and she was going to have a concert with him or without him. She'd have her birthday without Connar's help too. Connar was never going to fall in love with her now. All those girls, and he'd marry one of them, even though he said he'd never marry.

When she left the house she was wearing the dress she'd planned to wear for her birthday, her tears dried,

but still choking on the occasional sob. She went to
the ferry dock on Thetis Island and left on the very
first ferry of the morning. She didn't tell Aunt Jessie,
because she knew she'd be forbidden. She left before
Aunt Jessie was awake. She had enough money, just
enough. Enough for the bus and the big ferry over to
Vancouver, although she hadn't enough to get back
afterwards and she didn't care.

She wasn't coming back, she decided.

She'd been to Vancouver with Connar and Aunt
Jessie often enough to be able to get around on the
bus. She found the concert hall three hours before the
concert was to start. There was a park across the street,
and she went to sit there on a park bench. Sitting alone
in the park felt a lot more lonely than she had expected. When the concert was over she'd be stuck in
Vancouver, shivering in the park. She realised how
stupid she'd been. Connar always said she'd better
learn to think before she acted, and she hadn't done
that at all. She'd thought vaguely of getting a job,
but she had no idea how she'd go about doing that.
Maybe she'd even thought that her father would learn
she'd run away, that he would come because he cared
about her.

She hadn't seen him in over a year, and it was
getting hard to believe he really cared at all. She
thought about phoning Aunt Jessie, but she knew she'd
be in trouble. And Connar—he'd be out with
the girl again.

She wore a light raincoat against the cloudy sky. It
was winter, and threatening rain. Sitting on the park
bench, she was aware of the chill penetrating through
to her bones. After the concert she would go to the

bus depot and sit on a bench until morning. Bus terminals stayed open all night, didn't they? Then she'd . . .

She gulped and wondered what she would do. The idea of sitting alone in the bus terminal all night scared her. She shivered again and thought about Aunt Jessie, and knew she'd be worried sick by now. She'd have to phone her and she'd have to call collect.

Then she looked up and Connar was walking towards her. He was dressed in a lined overcoat that made his shoulders seem massive, corduroy trousers showing under the coat. His blond hair was darkened by the grey winter skies, the waves gone wild in the wind.

'Conn . . .'

He was glaring at her, walking towards her fast, as if he thought she might run. 'Mom's worried sick,' he growled when he got to her. 'What sort of stunt is this?'

She blinked hard and the tears spilled over. He sat down beside her on the bench and touched her shoulder. His touch broke a sob from deep inside her.

'Come on, Dix . . .' He pushed a handkerchief into her hand, and she used it to blot the tears. 'You're wearing mascara,' he said. 'It's smudging.'

She gulped, and felt agonisingly aware of her awkwardness.

'Why did you pull a stunt like this?' he demanded gently. He took the handkerchief from her and carefully cleaned her cheek under her left eye.

She shivered deeply. 'It's my birthday,' she whispered. 'He always called before. He always—he promised me.'

Connar pushed the handkerchief back into his pocket. 'He has to give up his time off when the news breaks. You know that.'

'Yes. I wrote to him,' she whispered. She stared down at her hands. 'Last month I wrote and asked if I couldn't go live with him like we used to when Mommy was alive. Do you think that's why he didn't come? Because he didn't want——'

'You're better off staying with Mom.' He touched her shoulder. 'Do you have the concert tickets?'

She nodded.

'Two of them?'

She nodded again.

'Let's go to dinner first.' He stood up and held out a hand towards her. 'We'll call Mom from the restaurant and tell her you're OK.'

'You're coming to the concert with me?'

He smiled then. 'Sure. It's your birthday, isn't it?'

In that moment it became a magical birthday. Walking with Connar to his car. Watching him as he drove through Vancouver's traffic with casual skill. Sitting across a table from Connar in an elegant dining-room, music in the background and Connar's voice washing over her. She was dressed for the celebration her father had forgotten, but that didn't matter any more. With mascara and lipstick on and a skirt that settled silkily around her when she sat, she had little trouble pretending that she was older.

Her fifteenth birthday, a candlelight dinner and the magic of Connar talking and listening to her as if her every word counted. She vowed to learn about the things he talked of, world trends and where the twenty-first century might take them.

After dinner he sat quietly with her through the concert, although when she glanced sideways at him she thought he looked as if he'd rather be doing something more active.

He took her to a hotel when the concert was over, signed her in, and left her at the lift in the lobby. 'I'll pick you up at ten in the morning,' he said. He would be driving her back home, taking his car on the ferry to Vancouver Island and then to the small community of Thetis Island.

'Connar?'

'Hmm?'

He had held her hand climbing steep hills. He'd dragged her home when she stayed out too long. Now he'd saved her from her own foolishness when she'd run away with no real objective in mind. She thought he still saw her as a kid, but she vowed one day that would change.

She tangled her hands together and felt embarrassment rising in her face. 'Could you—would you kiss me...for my birthday?'

'Sure.' He pressed his lips briefly to her cheek. 'There'll be a message from your dad when you get home, you know.'

'What's your girlfriend's name at the university?'

'Why?'

'Is it Elsie?'

'Forget Elsie.' His lips twitched in a half-smile. 'You were right. Too much hairspray.'

Her fingers tightened together. 'Is there another girl?'

'There are always girls,' he said soberly. 'But I'm not planning to get tied down.'

She huddled in the massive hotel bed that night and wondered about his girls. Lots of girls was better than only one, but it would be a long time before she could hope for him to look at her as anything but a child. Sixteen wouldn't be old enough. He'd be twenty-three then, and he'd still think she was a kid. Eighteen, maybe, or nineteen.

She had always watched the news to see her father's broadcasts, but now she began to watch for knowledge, to learn the things that interested Connar. She used her baby-sitting money for subscriptions to *Time* magazine and *Maclean's*. She read them, frowning and sorting out the details, so that when Connar came home for Easter that year she asked him what he thought about the latest hostage-taking incident in the Middle East, and he glanced at her with surprise.

'I'm just interested,' she said.

She was painting a water-colour of Telegraph harbour when he arrived that Easter. He spent hours lazing in the easy-chair in the attic-room she'd been using as a studio, talking and watching her paint. Before he left he talked with the owner of a small crafts store on the island. 'They'll hang that painting when it's done,' he told her. 'Who knows? It might sell.'

Dixie finished the painting in April and was thrilled when it sold to a tourist in the first week of June. She began thinking about art college instead of university. She would be seventeen when she graduated from school, and Connar wouldn't think about having an affair with a seventeen-year-old girl, much less marrying one.

The next year she went to Connar's university graduation with Aunt Jessie. Her father was there too. It was one of his rare visits. He shook Connar's hand and said, 'I expect to be seeing a lot of you over the next few years.' He seemed as proud of Connar as if he were his own son. To Dixie her father seemed a stranger, a man she knew better on television than in person. She loved him and of course he loved her too, but she thought she would probably never know him any better than she did now.

Her father flew to New York two hours after Connar's graduation ceremony. The next day Conn flew to Toronto, where he had been offered a job with CBC television. At the airport when Dixie asked him whether she would see him on the news, he laughed.

'I start at the bottom. You'll have to wait for me to get to the top.' He chuckled at the sober frown she gave him, then he leaned forward and gave her a light kiss on her cheek. It was a ritual that had started on her fifteenth birthday. A big-brother kiss.

But one day he would give her a real kiss.

She knew a different Connar in her fantasies, a lover like the men in the novels she had begun to read. One day she would be a woman and Connar would fall in love with her.

She graduated from high school when she was seventeen, a magic ceremony with everyone she loved watching as she went up for her diploma—Connar and Aunt Jessie and even her father. Connar had taken a new job with Continental Television's Los Angeles bureau, and her father had just been posted back to the Paris bureau after two years in Tokyo—

but they both came for Dixie's graduation. After the ceremony she danced with her father, then with Connar, who held her too impersonally, but at least said he approved of her plan to go on to art college. She told herself there was something different in Connar's eyes as he watched her that day, a new awareness in his arms as they held her to dance.

If so, it wasn't enough to stop him returning to Los Angeles the next day, or to prevent his coming to the farm the next Christmas with a sultry blonde on his arm.

'Sonya Curtland,' he said, introducing her.

Sonya smiled as if for a camera, but she had eyes only for Connar. Predatory eyes.

'If he marries *her*,' muttered Aunt Jessie, 'we're in for trouble.'

After that Christmas vacation Dixie went back to art college in Vancouver. Connar and Sonya returned to LA. Dixie was old enough now to understand that Conn and that woman were lovers. In the weeks that followed she faced the fact that her childish dreams of Connar were only that—impossible dreams. She would never find entry to his world. He would never look at her the way he'd looked at Sonya.

She painted and sketched her way through her next term in a black misery. Connar made three brief trips to Vancouver that year. Each time he managed a day with his mother on Thetis Island and a few hours with Dixie. In between visits he sometimes called on the telephone. She listened to his voice and exchanged news with him, but she knew his calls for what they were. He cared about her, yes. Like a brother or a cousin. Not the way she'd dreamed.

She got a part-time job in an art gallery, and with work and art college and her new friends she became as busy as Connar and her father. She had begun to date, and she was popular. She only got home to Thetis Island for the occasional weekend. She saw her father on her nineteenth birthday because she flew to visit him in Paris—the trip a gift from her father.

In her third year at college a law student who lived in her boarding-house asked her out. He was tall and blond, and the first time she saw him on the stairs she thought it was Connar and her heart stopped. Yes, she said, and over the weeks that followed she began to think she could fall in love with Jason Ellers.

When Aunt Jessie told her that Connar was bringing the blonde Sonya home for Christmas again, Dixie invited Jason. Connar frowned when he met him, but it obviously wasn't jealousy, because the next morning he took Jason for a walk alone along the beach, and later he told Dixie, 'He's OK.'

On the way back to Vancouver Jason told Dixie he was glad he had only honourable intentions, because he wouldn't want to face Connar Stanford otherwise. Jason took her out dancing on New Year's Eve. He was graduating from law school in a few months, and five minutes after midnight he asked Dixie if she would marry him the week after graduation. Yes, she said. She called Connar the next day to tell him.

'You'll be living in the city,' he warned her, his voice distorted by interference on the long-distance line. 'Jason's OK, but you were never meant to live in the city forever. Wait a few years, Dix. Be sensible. Finish college. Don't rush into anything.'

'What about Sonya?' she asked. She gripped the receiver hard. 'Will you marry her?'

'I'm going to Europe next month,' he told her, as if it were an answer. 'I'll be a correspondent at the Paris bureau.'

'Sonya's not going?'

'No,' he said, which meant Sonya had been temporary and probably there would be another woman in Paris.

'Will you come to my wedding?' she asked in a brittle voice.

'Put it off a couple of years, Dix. You're only twenty.'

She cried when she hung up the phone. Connar didn't care at all if she was in love with Jason. 'Be sensible', he said, but he liked Jason. Yet when he'd said he was going to Paris Dixie had known that if he said, Come to Paris; I want you, she would have thrown up her art course and Jason and everything.

The next day she told Jason that she couldn't marry him.

She couldn't marry a man whose main attraction for her was waving blond hair and broad shoulders, a fleeting resemblance to Connar, who was going to the other side of the world and wouldn't miss her much when he was gone.

One morning in early April Aunt Jessie went out to work on her garden. Hours later a neighbour found her lying between the furrows of freshly turned earth. A heart attack.

Connar flew home from Paris the next day. Dixie's father sent flowers.

Before he returned to Europe, Connar took Dixie out to dinner. 'I've hired Evan Collinson to look after the farm,' he told her. 'He's been Mom's hired hand for years and he knows the place. Maisie will keep the house in shape.' He was talking quietly, sitting across the table from her in a dining-room on Vancouver's waterfront. 'You and Mom talked about your coming home to live after you finished art school. I'd like you to do that, Dix. You could paint there, sell your stuff to the tourists in the local gallery.' He made a gesture that somehow sketched the emptiness of the Thetis Island farm without his mother. 'She'd want you to make your home there. I want that too.'

'Yes,' she said, 'thank you.' She wanted to tell him she was sorry, that Aunt Jessie had been the only mother she'd had since she was very small. She didn't know what words to use, and in the end they parted without the words being said. He kissed her cheek and she cried alone in her room because the only family she had left—Connar and her father—were a world away and only accessible on her television screen.

Dixie started her last year of art college in September living in two realities. She was twenty years old and she felt unreal, the engagement with Jason gone as if it had never been, the woman who had taken the place of her mother gone forever except in memory. She buried herself in her studies, in painting a large water-colour of the Granville Island market where the art college had a studio.

And she watched television. Not the network news broadcasts, but the feeds. The apartment where she lived had satellite television, and Dixie knew from her father and Connar the times when the news was often fed from Europe to the different networks in North America. They were raw news feeds, destined to be cut and edited before they came on the regular news broadcasts. Connar had called them 'wild feeds'. She watched to catch those precious moments before the interview started—Connar or her father chatting to someone on the other side of the world, the sounds blanked out, but the faces live. Or sometimes simply standing idle, waiting for the signal that would come in the headphones. Both men seemed very real to her in those seconds of waiting transmitted from the other side of the world, footage destined to be cut before the official news was aired.

She was watching the wild feed from Paris on the last day of September, watching her father standing on the pavement in front of a large house where terrorists held a family hostage. Behind her father she could see a confusion of police and officials.

There were seven people held at gunpoint in that house, her father said. She saw him shift as if to shelter himself from a cold wind. He looked thinner. Older. This year in early December she would go to Paris again for her birthday. This time she would also stay for Christmas, because there would be no Christmas celebration at the farm on Thetis Island. She already had her tickets for the flight and she was looking forward to it, wondering if she would see Connar while she was there.

She heard a dull popping sound from the television. Then another, the same. She saw Devlin Bradshaw's eyes widen in shock in the timeless instant before his lean body collapsed. A heart attack, she thought. Just like Aunt Jessie. She pushed out of the chair and was halfway across the living-room in an instant, as if she could reach him. As if she could help him. Then a voice she didn't recognise shouted over her television speaker.

'Gunshots! They got Dev!'

She'd seen violence on television before, but it had always been other people's tragedies. Unreal. 'Gunshots', the voice said, but she'd heard only popping sounds that were nothing like how she'd imagined a bullet firing would sound. She saw a man hurrying towards her father's body. Connar. He was there on that street in Paris. She saw his back as he crouched down beside her father, and she told herself it would be all right. Connar was there.

Then the camera swung wildly and the feed went dead.

Dixie sat in her living-room, knowing there was no one she could call, no way she could get information. Connar was with her father. Connar would call when he could. She didn't want to tie up the telephone, but she made one quick call to a travel agent. She made a reservation on the next available flight to Paris— the following day. If her father was in hospital she would be there to visit him.

Then she waited. Connar would call. She believed that, she trusted him, and she waited, watching the satellite channel where nothing came. Later she switched to a news network and heard an announcer say without inflexion that a network correspondent from the Paris bureau had been gunned down by terrorists. They gave no names and no information, and they didn't show that footage she'd seen again—her father falling in mid-word with the sound of popping around him.

Her telephone rang. She picked up the receiver and sat shivering, with Connar's voice in her ear demanding, 'Are you alone, Dixie?'

She knew the truth then. She didn't need his words to know her father was dead.

'Tell me, Connar. Tell me...'

He told her with bare words said quickly, not drawing it out. There had been a gunshot from a terrorist, and he had died moments later. She sat shivering and numb.

'Is Sally at home?' he asked. 'Isn't it Sally who lives in the next apartment?'

She didn't want anyone. Only Connar.

'Dixie? Talk to me. Is Sally home?'

'I'll fly to Paris,' she said dully.

'No. I'll be with you the day after tomorrow. I'm bringing him back with me. Go next door to Sally's and ask her to be with you tonight, Dixie. As soon as you hang up. Will you promise me that?'

She was shivering, hurting inside. 'I need you,' she whispered.

'I'll be there,' he promised. 'I'll look after everything.'

Hours later a man from Foreign Affairs came to her door to tell her that her father had died from a terrorist's bullet on a street in Paris.

CHAPTER THREE

'I THINK it would be best if we got married.'

Dixie was coming into the living-room from her kitchenette when Connar said those words. She had a tray in her hands. 'Coffee?' she had offered. He hadn't answered, but she'd stumbled into the kitchen and fumbled with water and coffee grounds. She needed something to hold back the moment when feeling would come.

When she returned with the tray Connar was at the window with his head bent, so that she knew he was staring down at the street. He was ten feet away from her when he spoke those incredible words, not looking at her. From the remoteness of his voice he might have been on the other side of the world.

Dixie clutched the tray. They had been talking about her future only a moment ago. 'What will you do?' he had asked. 'What are your plans?'

'I'll finish art school,' she had answered dully. 'I've this year to finish. I'm not sure—I might have to get a job if there isn't money.'

'Surely your dad left life insurance?' She hadn't looked at his face, but she'd heard the frown in his voice.

'I suppose . . . I don't know.' She had shrugged. 'I can work at the gallery full-time if I have to.'

He'd moved angrily, so that for a moment she'd thought he was angry at her. 'If there isn't enough . . .

If you want to finish art college, I'll make sure you
can do that.'

She had shaken her head and said, 'I can't take
money from you,' and he'd crammed his hands into
the pockets of his trousers with a violence she didn't
comprehend.

'Why not?' he'd demanded.

'I... Do you want coffee?' She'd fled into the
kitchenette then, returning only when the coffee was
ready. That was when he'd spoken quietly without
even looking at her.

'You'd accept my help if we were married. I think
it would be best if we got married.'

She clutched the tray and stared at his back, willing
him to say the words again. A man didn't ask a woman
to marry him with his back turned and his voice a
million miles away. He turned to face her, and she
must have spent too many hours watching him on
television. Somehow she had the wild conviction that
the television image was the reality and this scene in
her apartment the fantasy.

Or perhaps nothing was real. Her father gone and
Aunt Jessie buried last spring. The farm on Thetis
Island looked after by neighbours and Connar a
stranger from her television—except that he was *here*.
She could feel his restlessness, and when he moved
she could smell the clean scent of his maleness. He
made her bachelor suite seem crowded even while his
prowling vitality pulled her pulse faster.

'I know it's the wrong time,' he said. She gulped
and tried to read his eyes, and found nothing. 'I can't
stay long, Dixie. I'll have to go back to Paris in a few
days. You're in no shape to be making decisions. I

know that.' She saw him survey the room with those
eyes that missed nothing. Then his gaze met hers again
and he said, 'I can't leave you here alone. And I think
we could do a reasonable job of making a marriage.'

'I—why?' He didn't answer, and she said almost
angrily, 'I'll be all right without... I'm not a child,
Conn.'

For just a second his eyes were hot on her, sweeping
over the curves hidden by her loose clothing. She felt
herself flushing, and confusion followed, because
she'd never thought he looked at her and felt anything like what was in his eyes in that second. Then
it was gone, and he bent to pick up a clay figure she
had fired last week in the college's kiln. A killer whale,
not painted yet. He turned the little figure in his hand.

'You've been alone too much. You're not looking
after yourself. And I...' He put the killer whale down
carefully. 'There's no one else, is there?' He lifted his
head and pinned her with his gaze. 'Jason was at the
funeral. The way he was watching you... Are you in
love with him?'

'No.' She gulped, and wondered why she was so
scared when he'd just asked her to marry him and
she'd dreamed of this for years. He came to her and
took the tray out of her hands. She stared at him as
he put it down on the coffee-table.

'I know it's the wrong time, Dixie, but it's the only
time I've got.'

'We're friends.' She tried to swallow a hard lump
of panic. 'You never wanted—you never kissed me
or...'

He reached out and touched her hair. She stood
motionless with his hands threading through her hair

and his eyes intent. 'I can't leave you here, Dixie, going off to class every day and coming home to this empty place. You told me last year that you hated the city, that you were only here because of the art college. And now...' He made an angry gesture that reminded her of a younger Connar, angry because a neighbour's boy had bullied her, Connar looking after her as if she were the most important person.

'I can't leave you here,' he muttered. 'Not like this, alone in the midst of two million people.' He slid his hands down her arms lightly, a caress that left her nerves screaming. 'Come with me, Dixie. Come back to Europe with me.'

She didn't know what words to say. He was the only person she had left in the world, but she was afraid to ask him why he wanted this. Why *now*?

'But you don't—we've never...' She gulped.

'But we could,' he said gently.

He cupped his hands around her face and slowly lowered his mouth to hers. She stared up at him until his face blurred out of focus. Then his lips were on hers, and she felt the softness of her mouth giving way under his kiss. His mouth was gentle but not gentle. His hands slid away from her face and moulded her back. When he drew her close she could feel his body, and she'd dreamed of this, but the reality made her tremble, and a broken cry whispered from her mouth.

His tongue found entry to her mouth. She felt her body weaken and melt against his. He took her weight while his lips gently drew out the pain of the last few days. Then he took his mouth away, and her body was trembling and her face covered with silent tears. He stared down at her.

'You see,' he said gently, 'it could work. We're already friends, and I promise you this part of it will work. You're a beautiful woman and you don't find me unattractive, do you?' His hands caressed her back once more and sent a fresh wave of weakness through her.

She whispered, 'You said you weren't going to marry.'

'Marrying you is different.' He tangled her hair with his hands, twisting it around his fingers to bring her mouth back to his. 'You know what to expect in the life I lead. You'll understand about my job...and I refuse to leave you alone here.' He brushed the hard coolness of his lips across hers. 'I'll look after the licence.'

It was her dream, but she'd imagined happiness, not tears on her face from her father's funeral. But there was also the seductive lethargy from his kiss, from the sensation of his hands, gentle on her.

'I don't... Connar, are you sure?'

'I'll look after everything. I'll look after you. And if you want to study art, what better place than Paris?'

She shivered. 'Conn? Do you love me?'

He caressed her cheek with his thumb. 'I care about you and I'm not going to leave you like this.' His thumb grazed her chin. 'I know it's a bad time for you. I won't expect anything of you. I won't push you for anything you're not ready to give.'

She moved through the next few days mechanically, expecting at any moment to discover that none of it was true, that her father hadn't been buried, that Conn hadn't asked her to marry him.

Marriage. This was the wedding she had dreamed of, except that it was going to be held in the shadow of sadness from her father's funeral. 'I'll look after you', Connar had said. But he hadn't said he loved her. He cared about her. But caring was love, wasn't it? You didn't marry without loving. Especially Connar, who had once vowed he would never marry at all.

At least her passport was current. The rest didn't seem to matter. Connar had said he would look after everything and, although she knew she had to give notice to her landlord and the art school, she couldn't seem to make herself get in motion.

She hadn't seen much of him since he announced that they should marry. He'd got the licence, then disappeared for two days while he made a quick flight to New York, where he had to meet with someone at his network. Their life would be like that. Even in Paris he would be flying away at a moment's notice, but he would come home to her.

He loved her. Why else would he marry her? And if he loved her he would always come back to her. She told herself that, but she felt frozen inside. She had tried to tell Connar that it would be better if they waited. It wasn't fair to marry him when part of her was frozen inside. She'd dreamed of being his wife ever since she was old enough to have romantic dreams, but in her dreams she'd been loving and laughing, not frozen with grief over her father, so that he had to be careful of her, so that he frowned when he looked at her and promised her he wouldn't push her.

She tried to make herself come alive, but she felt as if she were surrounded by a thick layer of cotton. She couldn't seem to feel anything. The only thing she felt was when he held her in his arms and kissed her, and he'd only done that the once, when he'd said they should marry.

She woke in darkness the last night before the wedding. She sat up and felt the terror of a cold sweat, her own cry echoing in the empty room. Connar's name was on her lips, and her father's. She sat with the covers twisted around her, her body trembling, and the images as real as they could be. That scene back in Paris, transmitted by satellite. Shivering in her narrow bed in the middle of her last night as a single girl. She felt the dream around her, and it was truth mixed with horror. Her father struck down while she watched. Connar... She felt the tears on her face and heard her own sobs as she cried in earnest, grieving her father's death.

What if one day she saw Connar die?

Marriage. Until death us do part. He cared about her. He was her dream, but in the dream he loved her. Marriage, he'd said, but, shivering in a tangle of bed-clothes, she knew she'd been frozen ever since she watched her father fall to a terrorist's bullet on television. She had accepted everything Connar suggested without questioning, and she was frightened.

It was too sudden. He'd treated her like a sister, and now he'd asked her to marry him, but he'd hardly touched her since that one kiss. In church you promised love forever, but he'd intended a register office wedding until she'd protested. Would he mean it when he promised to love her until death? She'd heard him say more than once that he didn't believe in the forever kind of love.

But if he promised in church...

He hadn't wanted a church service. Her mind kept coming back to that.

He telephoned at nine in the morning. 'Is everything OK?' he asked briskly, as if calling her were an item on a list he'd made.

'Yes,' she lied.

'I've been on to the network,' he told her. 'I can take a few days more. We'll go to Thetis Island.'

She didn't answer. She'd asked if they could go to the island, and he'd said if there was time.

'Dixie?'

'I'm here.' She gripped the telephone receiver hard.

'Dixie, do you want to call this off?'

She wanted to slow it down. She wanted to know what he really felt for her. 'No,' she whispered. 'I don't want to call it off.'

A pause, as if he was evaluating words before he spoke. 'I promise you, Dixie, it'll be all right.'

It was a quiet ceremony. She heard her own voice in the small chapel and it sounded clear and certain, as if she knew what she was doing. Perhaps she did. She was marrying Connar Stanford, and she'd loved him since she was a little girl. The scary feelings inside her were because she would have to do so many things in an awful hurry—things she should have been doing while Connar took that flight to New York, like packing and vacating her apartment and telling them at the art college why she hadn't been to a class for a week and wouldn't ever be there again.

She was going to Paris with her husband.

She remembered the time when she'd come upon him with Elsie on the beach all those years ago. She remembered how they'd been kissing. Connar hadn't kissed Dixie like that. Not yet. He'd kissed her lips and touched her body gently as if to reassure her that she would respond to his loving. But he'd been in control. Not like that time in the grass with Elsie. Dixie remembered the urgency she'd sensed in Connar in that instant, the way his shoulder muscles were bunched up. She'd slipped away and then she'd run, but she'd remembered. And years later when she'd learned about lust between a man and a woman she'd understood.

If Connar felt that sort of desire for Dixie he managed to control it very well. He'd said he wouldn't expect anything of her, as if he thought she didn't want loving because she was too deep in her grief. She thought his touch might have made her feel less alone, more as if this marriage were real.

But they were real words she said in the church. 'I will'. He said them too. She listened, and his voice was strong and serious. 'I will,' he said, and surely that meant he loved her.

He placed a gold ring on her finger. He'd looked after buying the ring in the same way he'd looked after everything else, but she didn't have a ring for him. She should have told him she wanted a double ring ceremony just as she had said she wanted a church ceremony. That and their going to Thetis Island were the only things she'd asked for, and he had given her both.

A ring on his finger might make her believe it was true.

He kissed her when the vows were over. His lips were undemanding, as if to tell her that even with his ring on her finger he would not pressurise her to be a real wife. He was willing to let her go on being non-functional as long as she needed.

She wished he'd ask something of her. She wished he would kiss her as if he wanted more than that chaste pressure of lips, wished he would kiss her as he had kissed Elsie when he was a boy of seventeen.

They went to her apartment from the church. 'I haven't packed,' she apologised.

'I'll look after it,' he said.

He'd been saying that for days. She wanted to tell him to stop. It made her feel as if he were looking after a child. She was twenty, a married woman now. He'd squeezed three extra days from his busy schedule so that he could take her to Thetis Island. At the very least she could have packed her own apartment up.

'I just packed a small suitcase,' she said, gesturing to where she'd put the case earlier that morning. 'For a couple of days...'

He looked at it soberly. 'Are you sure you want to go to Paris with me?'

She gulped and could not get any words out. He reached down and picked her case up. 'Don't worry about it now. Let's get you to the island, where you can relax.'

Somehow it was easier then. He sat beside her on the familiar ferry ride to Vancouver Island and told

her about a river ferry he'd taken once in South
America. She shuddered as he described the insects
in graphic detail, and when he smiled she managed a
laugh. She saw his eyes warm with her laughter and
she told herself then that it was going to be all right.
Real vows. To love. To honour. To cherish. He was
waiting for her to be ready, that was all. She should
be glad he wasn't the sort of man to take advantage
of her grief.

They stopped for dinner at a quiet restaurant on
Vancouver Island. They had espresso coffee afterwards, and Connar asked her about her clay mod-
elling and her paintings.

'I'm experimenting with doing portraits with lamp-
black,' she told him. 'I like the effects I get with it.'
He listened and asked questions, and they stopped at
a gallery, where they argued about the merits of the
paintings hung there with an easy camaraderie.

It was all right. Millions of women would give anything for a husband as considerate as Connar. He had
come halfway around the world because she needed
him, and he was taking her home with him.

It was just before dark when they boarded the little
ferry that would take them to Thetis Island where it
nestled against the coast of the larger Vancouver
Island.

'I'm glad we're going to the farm,' Dixie said. They
were standing on the deck of the ferry, watching as
the island's shadow loomed closer. 'It's my favourite
place.'

Connar gave her a sharp look and she flushed, because he was taking her to Paris and she was talking
as if she wanted a different sort of home. And it was

true that she would prefer life here on this island—if Connar could be with her. This was her real home, but she knew Conn would never stay in this place where news was only something you saw on television.

Wherever Connar lived would be her home. Perhaps one day when they had children...

They drove the island road to the farmhouse in silence. Then Connar got out and opened her door, and she stood quietly while he got their suitcases from the trunk. They walked side by side to the farmhouse where they'd both grown up. Quiet. Empty house. Dixie couldn't remember ever returning to this house without Aunt Jessie somewhere within shouting range.

'I told Evan we were coming,' Connar said. 'He was going to lay in some food.'

'Aunt Jessie...' She closed her eyes, and she felt the same thing he must be feeling. 'I feel as if she's going to call out to us any minute.'

Connar put the bag down. 'You miss her.'

'Yes. So do you.'

He stared at the suitcase he'd set on the floor. She'd had this fantasy that he would carry her over the threshold, but maybe that happened when he got her to the place where they would live. Or maybe he thought that sort of thing was silly.

She followed him when he took her case upstairs. He put it into the room she had always slept in, her childhood room. He put his bag in his room. Separate rooms. She went into hers and closed the door. He meant them to sleep alone tonight. She'd been counting on darkness to bring them together, to lead her into intimacy with her husband. Didn't he want her? He was friendly to her, but when she looked into his eyes she saw nothing like the desperation she felt when she thought of him going away and herself left behind.

She opened her suitcase and began to unpack.

Then she changed out of the clothes she'd travelled in.

He was downstairs when she came out of her bedroom. She stood in the corridor in a moment of panic and uncertainty. Should she go downstairs? She wrapped her arms around her waist, as if the warm September evening had turned chilly.

The door to his bedroom was open.

She walked slowly into his room. The floor felt cool under her bare feet. She'd been in here years ago, had sprawled on the bed and chattered while Connar built models or tried to study. She could remember her voice rising as she'd told him about problems at school, her plans for her birthday when her father came. She had told him about her dreams, how she was going to be a great painter one day. He'd never laughed at her, although he must have had his doubts. In turn she'd listened to his dreams and known that Connar would make his plans for the future into hard reality.

She wondered what they would talk about in the years to come, whether he had new dreams now that he'd achieved that old ambition. He'd dreamed of being like her father, although it had never seemed to be the fame he wanted. He'd wanted to be there, to see the shape of history being formed. He'd achieved his dream, and now she would be with him. At his side.

She stood at the window, staring out on darkness, with her ears stretched for his sounds. In a few days she would be following him into a strange new life. He thought she was accustomed to being in a newsman's family, but she hadn't lived with her father since she was six years old, and she wasn't sure what Connar expected of her.

He seemed to have no expectations of her body. He had only taken that one kiss, that heating embrace that he'd broken off on the day he asked her to marry him. She kept reminding herself that Connar had seemed certain that they would suit each other in the physical part of marriage. But how could he know? And what if he had ushered her into her old room because he himself had doubts? What if he realised he'd just made a mistake, but he wasn't going to tell her yet? He was being very careful of her because she'd just lost her father.

She froze when she heard his footsteps on the stairs. He had been moving about downstairs as if he was locking windows and checking doors. Now he was coming upstairs. She stared through his window at a spot where a light from the neighbours' farm sent a circle of warmth through the trees. She heard him walking closer, along the corridor outside his room, then into the room. Then she heard the instant when he stopped moving.

She turned around slowly. She should have faced him as he came into the room. Whatever he'd thought when he first saw her waiting in his bedroom dressed in filmy lace, that thought was hidden from her forever now.

'Dixie...' He came two more steps into the room and stopped again. His face was tense. Unrevealing. 'You don't need to do this,' he said.

She stepped towards him. He was wearing trousers and the white silk shirt he'd worn to marry her. He must have discarded his jacket and the tie downstairs. She bent her head and stared down at her own hands, clenched together in front of her. Her wedding-ring showed as a bright gold band between her folded fingers.

'Why not?' she asked. Her voice was constricted. 'We are married, aren't we?'

His hands clenched at his sides. She glanced up hurriedly, and he was staring at the froth of lace where the nightgown crossed her bodice. 'Give it time,' he said. His voice sounded odd. Strained.

'Are you sorry you married me?' she demanded on a whisper that cracked.

He muttered something, and for an instant she thought he was going to touch her, and it would be in anger to echo the sudden frustration in his voice.

'Conn...?'

'I don't expect a bloody sacrifice, Dixie.'

She gulped and wanted to tell him it wasn't a sacrifice. She needed his arms around her, but, staring into his face, she was becoming more and more frightened.

He brushed at the hair on his forehead with one hand. 'I'm not crazy about standing here staring at you in that excuse for a gown. It looks as if it would——' his voice broke and he cleared his throat roughly '—would come undone if I just pulled on that——'

'Conn,' she whispered. 'Please . . .'

'Where did you get that?' He gestured to the bow of satin that held the gown closed. 'Did you wear it for Jason?'

'Conn, I . . .'

His eyes closed and he muttered hoarsely, 'You're not ready for this. Your father's funeral last week and . . . for God's sake get out of here before I . . .' He made a blind gesture, and when his eyes opened she felt her heart start to beat.

'Connar, please . . .' Aunt Jessie had never taught her how to handle this sort of situation. Jessie had been the loving mother Dixie remembered for most of her life, but she'd never told Dixie how to stand in front of the man she loved and give herself to him with any degree of grace or confidence.

She gulped and said clearly, 'Conn, please hold me.' She reached out, and his chest was hard. She spread her fingers out and felt his heat and the slam of his heart against his ribs.

'Please love me,' she whispered.

CHAPTER FOUR

THE prints she had intended to deliver on Saturday were still sitting in Dixie's hall cupboard on Monday morning. Ernie would be prowling the mall, muttering because he was out of the *Cat Girl* and *Ensenada Siesta* prints. Knowing she had no real choice, Dixie swallowed her ridiculous panic at the thought of facing Connar again and piled everything back into the van.

'Do you want me to come?' asked Sue. Jess had gone over to a neighbour's child's house to play, and Sue was standing at the doorway of her white-walled house, a beautiful young woman in her early thirties with an abundance of flaming red hair. She looked too vital for the cane she used. They'd spent Sunday together, sitting under a big beach umbrella, watching the slow surf sweep in down on the beach below Sue's house, watching Jess playing with her friends and Wolf at the water's edge. Several times through the day Dixie had restlessly prowled down to the water, and Wolf had torn back and forth between Jess and Dixie in excitement.

Swimming hadn't washed away the reality for Dixie. How could it when every time she looked at her daughter she saw Connar's eyes, when she knew Connar was just across the border and wouldn't leave until he got what he wanted?

60

What did he really want? An explanation, he'd said. And a divorce.

She managed to laugh at Sue's suggestion that she needed support. 'He'll know I'm scared if I bring reinforcements,' she said.

Sue nodded, which must mean that Dixie was doing a better job than she thought of pretending Connar didn't matter all that much. It was crazy—she was twenty-seven now. Too old to be frightened of a man she'd worshipped as a child, a powerful man who managed to have his way with presidents and terrorists alike.

'He's probably already gone back to Timbuktu,' Sue said, 'or wherever it is he belongs.'

Where did Connar belong? Once it had been Paris. She'd never got that far with him. Paris had been only a word, a dream she had once thought might come true. The dream had died early.

She piled the last three prints into the van, and at the last moment she let Wolf jump into the back. She'd named him Wolf when she and Jess first saw him scrounging food at the edge of the market in Ensenada, something about his lean hungriness speaking of the wild, even while his shaggy black and white coat spoke of ordinary mongrel dog. When they'd learned that he had no home, Jess had looked at her with yearning in her eyes, and they had taken him home and washed the wildness out of his fur, fed him until he grew smooth flesh to cover the ribs that had been showing as he scrounged in the market. Wolf was fiercely loyal to both her and Jess, and maybe he would provide some sort of subtle protection if she needed it today.

On Saturday night on Shelter Island she could have used Wolf to growl at Connar.

At the American border Dixie picked the wrong Customs booth. A young Hitler with delusions of power glared at her. 'Citizenship?' he snarled.

'Canadian.' She handed him her passport.

'What about the dog?'

He tangled her up in red tape for half an hour. She showed him her Mexican vehicle registration, Wolf's certificates from the Mexican veterinarian and a copy of a receipt from the lithographer who had done the prints she carried in her back seat—proving that they'd been lithographed in the US.

She was crazy to truck the prints back and forth across the border. She often had trouble enough with the originals she brought up from her cottage to the lithographer. She'd only carried these prints into Mexico because she'd been fleeing from Connar in a childish panic. Lord knew what Conn was thinking. She'd evaded his questions as if he were a physical threat to her. Connar was no fool. He must have sensed she was hiding something.

If Connar knew about Jess...

She drove along the freeway with her mind fifteen hundred miles to the north. Thetis Island. Back in Connar's bedroom in a brief lacy nightgown she'd bought because she'd wanted him to desire her.

Heat had flooded her face as he stepped back from her. His gaze swept down to the naked white of her thighs. She'd come across the hallway in bare feet and she felt painfully conscious of the contrast between the lacy film that covered her from shoulders to thighs and the gaucheness of bare feet and toes curling on the cold floor.

In the mirror of her room she'd looked and seen lace covering the parts of her body that she was accustomed to covering: breasts and the tender slight roundness of her abdomen; the trembling range of her midriff. All covered, just hinted at. She'd seen the white and that was right, because she was innocent. In the mirror with only the light from the bedside table behind her it seemed that he might think her beautiful tonight.

She was nervous. Trembling. Standing with his eyes on her, she realised that lace was hardly better than nakedness. Her breath caught as his eyes stilled. She looked down, the sweep of her gaze following the path of his. The lace had taken her shape in a way she hadn't noticed in the mirror. The hard peaks of her nipples showed plainly through their thin covering. She flushed at the explicit message revealed by the betrayal of her own body's arousal. She'd been waiting for him . . . imagining . . .

She wanted to run, to close her eyes so that she couldn't see that stillness in him. Everything quiet except his breathing, and he didn't want her. This wasn't what he'd planned, taking her here in his old room with her body covered in lace and him surprised because he hadn't expected her here. He was staring as if he'd never seen her before, but in years past she'd run in front of him often enough in nothing more than a bikini. Once she'd been brushing her teeth when she was thirteen, dressed in nothing more than panties and a training bra. She'd forgotten to lock the bathroom door and he'd opened it, said, 'Whoops!

Sorry, Dixie,' and he'd been gone, and she'd never felt self-conscious about it.

But now...

'Dix...do you know what you're doing?' His voice sounded odd, strained by emotion.

She swallowed panic and stepped close to him again. Her hand touched his chest and made contact with the slamming of his heart. Abruptly his eyes turned to blazing black. Her lips parted in a gasp as his hands locked on her upper arms. Instantly his harsh grip softened. She felt his thumbs move on the soft flesh at the front of her arms, saw his throat spasm as he swallowed. She put both her hands flat against his chest and stared at the breadth of it and the way her hands looked small and almost as white as his shirt. Then she looked up into his face. It was harsh and grim, his eyes a hot blue-black, blazing down on her.

'Dixie...' He breathed her name unsteadily. Then he pulled her close and buried his mouth in hers.

His lips were hard. Like his body. Her mouth took the shape of his, her body moulding to his masculine hardness as he pulled her close. She made some sound, a gasp or perhaps a moan of protest at the hard roughness of his body against hers. His mouth responded by shifting in some subtle way from harshness to seduction. He was caressing her lips, her mouth, his tongue dancing with hers in a sensuous caress that made her heartbeat pulse with the intensity of his touch.

When he took his mouth from hers she made a sound, as if his mouth leaving hers were a tearing of flesh. One of his hands was splayed against her back, fingers possessing and caressing through the thin lace of her gown. The other slid down to posses her hips, and she lost the place where her body ended and his began. Each ragged breath she took made a seductive motion of her breasts against his hard chest, her abdomen shaping to the pressure of his rigid body. He bent his head, and his lips found the tender flesh of her neck.

'I didn't mean this to happen,' he groaned against her throat.

She swallowed pain at the harshness in his voice. She pulled back and he gave her a few inches of freedom, the distance between his body and hers. Then he released her.

She trembled and bit her lip. 'If you don't want...' She'd made a fool of herself. His eyes were on her face, but she could feel the swelling of her breasts, the painful sensitivity of her nipples to the lace as she breathed in and out. 'Why did you marry me?' she wailed softly.

He placed one hand along the side of her face. His flesh felt cool against her cheek. 'What else could I do?' he asked huskily.

She pulled away. 'I don't understand...'

He possessed her face with both hands and drew her mouth back towards his. 'Don't go,' he whispered. He brushed his mouth on hers softly, again and again. She tried to stare up into his face, to understand what was in his eyes.

'Why...not? You don't want...'

His fingers stroked down along the side of her throat and brushed her flesh into aching tenderness. 'I want you to stay.' His hand touched the gold chain that she always wore around her throat, the gold cross

that had been her mother's. 'I want you,' he murmured as his fingers followed the edge of the lace
where it crossed over between her breasts. Then he
possessed the satin ribbon that held the gown fastened
below her bodice.

'Do you love me?' she whispered.

His knuckles were pressed against the underside of
her full breasts. She felt the pressure as they pressed
deeper, and she knew that in a second there would be
nothing to hide behind. She heard the satin sliding on
itself as the bow came undone.

'Where did you find this thing?' His hand was motionless on the satin tie that he'd pulled. The bow was
gone, leaving just the two ribbons of satin linked
loosely and the two sides of her lace gown hanging
loosely from the peaks of her breasts. He traced the
line of skin that was visible between the two sides of
the gown. His finger lightly took possession of the
line between her breasts, slipped over the loose ribbon
and over trembling flesh to her navel. He paused there
for an instant. Then as her flesh shuddered ahead of
his touch he drew the slow line down to the lacy barrier
of the gown's matching bikini panties. 'Where?' he
asked again, his voice ragged.

'On Robson Street.' Her voice was oddly clear.

'Who have you worn it for?' His finger sliced up
and hooked the loose loop of the ribbons. 'Was it for
Jason?'

She felt the air freeze in her lungs as he grasped the
ribbons with both hands. He was going to undress
her, to take off these scraps of lace. The slowness of
his hands on her was making her painfully aware of
how naked she would be, of the way the white of his

shirt and the tailored length of his trousers kept him behind a barrier. She shivered, and a confusion of emotions tumbled through her. Fear, because she had no choice but to love him while he had not admitted to loving her. Anger, because he was moving the satin ribbons so slowly, pulling the sides of her gown back with his eyes locked on the growing nakedness of her body. And all the while he was locked behind that silk shirt and those immaculately pressed dress trousers.

'Did you wear this for Jason?' he demanded harshly. He was staring at her breasts as the satin slid away from her nipples. His voice sounded ragged as he repeated, 'Did you?'

She shook her head mutely.

'He won't have you again,' Connar growled. He slid the gown back over her shoulders. The satin and lace pooled down on her arms, caught by her bent elbows, so that the lace made a frame below her naked breasts.

'He never did,' she whispered so faintly that he might not have heard.

His hands traced the slope of her shoulders and paused at the pool of lace. Then he caressed back up her arms and softly over the curve of her breasts. His voice slid over her with a soft threat.

'Don't ever wear it for anyone else.' His palms moulded the slopes of her breasts, the nervous trembling of her abdomen. 'All this . . . all of you belongs to *me* now.'

He picked her up. She could feel the pressure of his arms tangled with the lace as he carried her to his bed. She stared up at his face as he lowered her, and she saw heat and desire and a primitive statement of ownership. The caveman taking his possession into his cave. His hand possessed her breast, the thumb sliding over the hard peak of her nipple. She stared into his eyes, and when the sensation ripped through her body she saw its echo in his eyes.

'I love you, Connar.' She had to whisper those words. If he didn't love her... if he didn't answer... She couldn't possibly do this with him unless he really loved her. She stared up at him and she breathed, 'I've always loved you,' and her words were a plea for his love.

His silence went on too long. There was desire in his eyes, heat and passion. Not love. He sat beside her on the bed. She closed her eyes, because she could not bear the truth in his. She had to get up and leave this room and cross the hallway to her childhood bedroom. She had to tell him she'd made a mistake and they would have to undo the knots that tied them.

If he didn't love her...

'No,' he said, and he touched her so that her senses buried the pain in her heart. 'Open your eyes,' he demanded roughly, and when she did he bent down and caressed her breast with his tongue, a slow, moist seduction that left her struggling for air, her head spinning and her heart pounding. When he stopped she reached up and her fingers tangled in his shirt. She pulled herself up, half sitting as she fumbled for the hot flesh under the silk of his shirt.

He took her wrists in his hands and held them away from his chest, away from her body as he covered the peak of her other breast with his parted lips. He drew her softness deep inside his mouth. Her breathing turned to a groan. Her back arched, and when he let

her wrists free her fingers tore into the buttons that
held his shirt. She twisted against him for the touch
of flesh on flesh as he caressed her softly, until she
cried out and his touch turned deep and demanding.
He kissed her and stroked her and possessed the dark
secrets of her body, their sounds and their bodies
mingling together in a storm that had no ending.

Passion. Not love.

In the months and years that followed she tried to
remember each separate detail of that night. She knew
it was a mistake, but it was an addiction she could
not give up. She often woke in a haze of red passion
that left her whispering his name and reaching back
for his touch and the sounds that weren't words, and
the instant when he found the wild centre of her
woman's body and she breathed out a long deep need,
and later his body over hers and his hardness demanding entry and the moment she became his, and
the cry she couldn't hold back, and the long stillness
when he understood that there was no one else, had
never been anyone else. Not Jason. Not any man.

Connar was her first lover. Her only lover.

That had to be why she was still hung up about
Connar Stanford. She'd read enough about women,
about loving, to know that the man she'd married had
to have been an incredibly skilled lover to have left
her haunted with desire for him. Far better if he'd
been fumbling and inept and she were left with a
memory of pain and fear. Instead she had the dreams,
the heat of memory and breathless need. Even the
moment of pain when he'd taken her innocence was
like a brand on her, telling her that Connar was
her owner.

Nonsense! One night couldn't put a brand on a woman. She'd been telling herself that for years, and now she knew she should have done more than just lecture herself about him. She'd watched his image on television, dreamed his touch—all that when she should have been saying yes to some of the men who'd tried to reach for her.

She had tried. She'd gone out a few times, on dinner dates and one trip to the theatre, sometimes dancing. She'd invited one escort, Jake, back to the cottage on Sue's property after the theatre. Sue and Jess had been away on an overnight trip to Ensenada, and Dixie had offered Jake coffee and in her mind she had planned to offer more. But then he'd taken her into his arms and she'd frozen when his lips found hers. She had meant to say yes to his kiss, had planned to give herself in a desperate effort to forget the dreams that would not leave her alone—but her body had betrayed her.

'Who is he?' Jake had demanded.

'Someone I'll never see again,' she answered, but that was a lie, because she watched the news and she searched for him in crowds. And at night she remembered his passion and woke shivering in the aching memories. 'I'm sorry,' she told Jake. 'I was trying to forget.'

'You still love him.'

'No,' she said. She didn't love Connar, but she couldn't forget him either. It had never been *real* love, just a childish passion that betrayed her. And now it must have become an obsession, because she couldn't get him out of her mind or her life.

She didn't try dating after the fiasco with Jake. She wasn't free, but she wasn't married either. She wasn't sure what the vows she'd exchanged with Connar really meant any more. Connar had certainly only been saying words, reading lines. Perhaps she hadn't meant them either, although at the time...

Luckily she had her art, and she threw herself into that, working harder as success came to her, so that there was no time for a man in her life and no man allowed past the barrier she set around herself. Not even Connar.

She watched for Connar as she walked through the crowd at the mall, but there were only Monday morning shoppers, mainly women, and one mall security guard talking to Ernie.

Dixie arrived, breathless, with her armful of prints. Ernie and the security man both reached to help her, but she evaded their reaching hands and set the prints down against the display table.

'About time,' muttered Ernie. 'There are so many holes in this display it looks ridiculous.' He picked up the top two prints and carefully placed them up on the rack, his stocky body oddly graceful as he straightened them.

'I'd better get on,' said the security man. 'Would you believe someone locked all the cubicles in the men's toilet? Then they crawled out under the doors and left them locked! I'm on the track of the mad door-locker!'

Had Connar been back? Dixie couldn't bring herself to ask Ernie. She helped him arrange the display to accommodate the new prints, then went out for the second lot.

She had a long way to go, all the way to the end of the mall, where she'd parked below a row of ornamental trees to give Wolf the shade. She bent her head and walked fast, trying not to spill the bowl of water she was bringing back for Wolf.

'Sorry, fellow,' she told him when she found him standing with his head out of the partly open window of her van and his tongue panting. She opened the door and let him out. He bent down and attacked the water with messy enthusiasm.

'Just a few minutes and we'll go off to Shelter Island,' she promised him. 'Then you can go swimming.'

Shelter Island? No, not this time. She would find another place to let Wolf free in the water, because Connar had ruined Shelter Island for her—or perhaps she'd ruined it for herself, standing on a rock and staring at him, realising that seven years hadn't gained her any immunity to him.

'Back in,' she told Wolf. Wolf lifted his head, as if to tell her that he knew better than to think he'd get freedom in the madness of the city. She loaded up the last armful of prints and left Wolf staring after her through the partly open window as she headed back to the mall.

She was two steps inside the mall when she saw Connar. It was like a rerun of Saturday, but this time her feet kept moving because he'd seen her. And because she was getting angry.

Connar Stanford was not going to control her life again! She got three more steps before he blocked her path. She had to stop, but she wasn't letting him win even the smallest battle.

'What are you doing here?' she demanded.

He reached for the paintings, and she shook her head and stepped back.

His hand shot out and he gripped her arm. 'Watch out!' he snapped.

She heard the startled cry of a child behind her, then the toddler cannoned into the back of her legs.

'Sorry,' apologised the youngster's mother.

'My fault,' said Dixie. 'I'm sorry.' She smiled at the youngster while trying to twist free of Connar's grip on her arm. She couldn't pull away without smashing into the mother and child.

'Let go of me,' she muttered.

'Give me the paintings,' he demanded.

'They're prints, not paintings.' She felt stupid and ridiculously young, standing in front of him in sandals and shorts and an oversized T-shirt, holding a bundle of prints and arguing.

He took them out of her arms. She stood still, refusing to move when he started towards the display. 'Come on,' he demanded.

'No,' she snapped.

An elderly woman stopped to listen, staring from Conn to Dixie.

'If you're delivering the prints for me,' said Dixie, 'then I'll be off.'

'Try it,' he said in a voice that made her shiver, 'and I'll throw these prints in the dumpster outside.'

'You wouldn't!' She jammed her hands into the pockets of her shorts. 'What is it you want from me?'

'A rational conversation. Somewhere we can sit down and talk.' She realised that he was at a disadvantage with his arms full of her prints. 'You owe me

at least a few sentences over a meal. After all, you
are my wife.'

It wasn't true. Not in any real sense. She turned
away from his eyes and found herself staring into the
intense grey of the old woman's eyes.

'This is a private conversation,' she muttered.

She heard Connar's harsh laugh behind her. 'Don't
go away,' he said, and he strode off towards the
display.

'You're crazy,' whispered the old woman. 'Grab
him! Can't you see he's a man in a million?'

Dixie shook her head and followed Connar slowly,
her hands still deep in the pockets of her shorts. She
would talk to him. She'd sit down and eat with him,
but she was damned if he would pay for her meal!
Maybe she did owe him some sort of explanation, and
perhaps she would even tell the truth about why she'd
left. There might be healing in that. Release. An end
to the dreams and the nightmares. But she wouldn't
tell him about Jess—not while they were still legally
married.

She'd talk to him. Then, afterwards, she would go
home and pull the plug on the television. Sue had
been talking about buying a second set for her
bedroom. Dixie would make her a gift of the set she'd
used to follow Connar's journeys through excitement
and danger, get rid of it.

Ernie's eyebrows shot up when he saw Connar
carrying her prints. 'Guess you did get together
after all,' he said, frowning, as if he suspected
Connar's motives.

Dixie pulled her hands out of her pockets and moved to the display. 'I'll do this,' she said, taking a print from Ernie's hands.

'He bought the original of *Cat Girl*,' Ernie told her.

Her eyes met Connar's. His gave nothing away. 'A high price to pay for an hour's conversation,' she said. Her heart was pounding as she searched his eyes.

'Ready?' he asked.

She was never going to be ready for this. Face to face with Connar, his journalist's eyes probing for her secrets. Why had he bought that particular portrait? Was there any possibility that he knew? That he'd guessed?

'I've got Wolf in the van,' she said desperately.

His lips twitched. 'You've got a wolf in your van?'

'My dog.' Her lips curved in response to his before she could stop them. 'We—I named him Wolf. It's too hot out there to leave him, so I——'

'We'll go somewhere else.' He took her arm and she went two steps with him before she got her body to respond to her will and jerk free of his touch.

'I can walk on my own!' she snapped.

'Touchy,' he murmured, but he dropped his hand.

'Will I see you later?' Ernie called.

'No,' said Connar.

'Yes,' Dixie snapped. 'Your place, Ernie?'

'Right,' Ernie agreed.

She walked quickly, as if she could outpace Connar's long legs. He didn't touch her, but he was only eighteen inches away from her—half a yard of tense conditioned air between them. The doors to the outside slid apart as they approached. Dixie stopped abruptly. What if there was some clue inside her van that would tell him about Jess's existence? A doll or...

He touched her arm. 'Do you expect I'm going to attack you?'

Heat flooded into her face. 'I expect you'll try to get whatever it is you want.'

'Perhaps I want my wife back.' She knew he didn't mean that, because his voice was ice.

'I have the life I want,' she said. Her throat was dry and stiff. 'It doesn't include a husband.'

'What about a divorce?'

She shrugged. 'Go ahead.'

He slid one hand into the pocket of his trousers. 'Don't your lovers mind that you're married? Or don't you tell them?' His voice was slow, empty of visible intent. She'd heard that same voice on her television, with his words leading the unsuspecting into verbal traps.

She followed the direction of his gaze, and saw that her hands were trembling. 'You seem very certain that I have lovers, Connar.'

'You're not wearing your wedding-ring.'

'So? I took it off because I didn't want to be married to you.'

'What did you do with it?'

She would never tell him the truth—that the ring was lying safely in her jewellery box, that she'd tried to make herself get rid of it but couldn't.

'I threw it away,' she snapped.

In Connar's face she saw fury, sudden and terrifying. She gasped and jerked back, and in the instant she moved it was gone.

'This isn't the place for this conversation,' he said. She had to be wrong about his anger, because now his voice was level and faintly bored. His hand touched her back, and she stepped quickly through the doorway just as the doors started to close again. His voice followed her on to the pavement outside. 'What are you afraid of, Dixie?'

She stopped walking and turned back to stare at him, a handsome man with a face that showed both laughter and frown lines. A man who had known what he wanted from life even when he was a boy.

'I'm afraid of you!'

'That doesn't make a lot of sense,' he said quietly.

'Yes, it does.' She met his eyes militantly. 'You've always managed me. When you didn't like the way I behaved you found a way to change it. When you wanted me to do something you found a way to make me do it.'

'You make me sound a bully.' A muscle jerked along the line of his jaw.

'A manipulator,' she corrected. 'You know how to get your way and you're used to getting it. So I suppose I'm afraid you can still make me do things I don't want to do. Like when I was a kid. The way you steamrollered me into marrying you. The way——'

'You were no child when you married me.' His nostrils flared, and for a second she saw the anger again. 'That was no child in my bed.'

'You have to poke at me, don't you?' she muttered. She knew he saw the heat flood over her face. 'Is that what this is about? A chance to take a shot at me, to embarrass me?'

He grasped her arms and shook them slightly. 'How long did it take you to break the vows you made in that church, Dixie? And why in hell did you marry me in the first place?'

'How long did you keep yours?' Her jaw went rigid. 'Or did you break them as you spoke the words?' One of her hands came free of his grasp, and she slid the door of the van open hard, so that it slammed against the stop. Wolf jumped out, and he growled threateningly at Connar.

'Call your dog off,' he said softly.

Wolf's canine body went rigid with tension as he emitted another threatening sound.

'Let go of me first,' she demanded huskily.

Conn's gaze bored into her eyes.

A staring match. Connar probably knew a lot more than she did about facing down threats, but Wolf's growl was sincere, and she wasn't speaking a re-assuring word to her dog until Connar's hands were off her body. And she wasn't letting herself remember how the touch of his fingers on her arm could turn her to liquid hunger!

'I'm not giving in,' she said.

The last thing she expected was that he would laugh, but he did. 'A Mexican stand-off,' he said softly. 'I'll give you this round.'

He opened the hand that held her arm and slowly stroked the warm naked flesh of her upper arm, sliding his fingers under the sleeve of her T-shirt before he stepped back. She was left with the echo of his light touch on her flesh, the responding sensation of fullness in her breasts.

'The dog's Mexican,' she said. Mercifully none of the huskiness in her throat managed to get into her voice.

She dropped her hand down to Wolf's head and scratched his ear. He leaned against her and she felt weak, as if the weight of the dog could make her sink to the pavement. As if Connar would watch, knowing it wasn't the dog at all, but the man's eyes on her.

The memories were too real. He'd mentioned their wedding night. He'd made that comment about her being no child, and she'd felt the flush of reality slipping away. She'd lost herself in the middle of one of those dreams where she was hungry and desperate and he stepped back from her and left her alone in a sensual fantasy-turned-nightmare.

'Mexican?' he asked. 'That's where you live, isn't it? Is that where you ran when you left me?'

'Yes.' Her fingers clenched in Wolf's fur. 'I thought you couldn't find me there.'

CHAPTER FIVE

WOLF dashed past Connar and leapt into the van, where he stood with his black tail wagging slowly and his eyes on Dixie. Connar moved towards the driver's door.

'You're not driving my van!' said Dixie.

'Then I hope you've learned a bit since you passed your road test.'

She would have liked to growl at him if she could do it without looking childish. 'The place I'm going isn't your style,' she muttered.

'Where?' he asked, and she realised that he was laughing at her. She got into the driver's seat and leaned across to let Connar in the passenger door. He glanced around the interior of the van as if he expected to find bits of trash and dust. She frowned and started the engine with a roar.

'A hamburger place,' she said.

'I've eaten in places that would make that seem like high cuisine,' he said mildly.

'You mean when the terrorists . . .' She glanced at his face and saw that he would not talk about that. She clenched her hands on the wheel. 'I was worried,' she said in a low voice. 'Every time you disappeared I was terrified.' Behind Connar, Wolf was standing with his tail wagging slightly, waiting for the van to start and the wind of motion to cool him. She drew her lower lip between her teeth. 'And you always

80

turned up laughing at death. As if you thought you were immortal.'

'If you were worried,' he demanded in a dry voice, 'why didn't you contact me?' She wouldn't let herself look at his face, but she knew from his voice how it would be. Alert. Watchful. 'You never did write or call,' he said.

'No,' she agreed.

'Didn't you think you owed me at least the re-assurance that you were still alive?'

Yes, of course she had owed him that, but... 'What was I to do? Call and say, "Everything's fine and I don't want to see you"? You promised my father you'd look after me.' She squeezed her eyes closed and whispered, 'I saw you go to him—you were beside him on the pavement. If he asked you to promise, it was then. While he was dying... Are you going to haunt me all my life because my father had a guilty conscience about me when he was dying?'

He touched her cheek lightly, shaking his head slightly when she jerked back from his touch. 'That footage was cut from the news broadcast in North America. How did you see it?'

'A wild feed on satellite. I saw... I...' She gulped and clenched her hand on the gearstick. 'Damn! I don't want to talk about that! I... At the burger place there's a park. We could eat outside and let Wolf run. There are picnic tables. And I... if——'

'I'm sorry,' he said gently. 'I asked Tom Gaylie to get it cut from the broadcast, and he agreed. I didn't want you to see it.'

She didn't look at him, didn't want to see what was in his face. This was the Connar she could not resist, the man who understood the things she didn't say. The man she'd once loved above all. She fired the engine and drove hard, pushing the old van to its limits, driving on the freeway when it would have been easier to drive through the city. When she got to the car park between the burger stand and the park she shoved the gearstick into first and killed the engine. It ran on a couple of cycles, as if it needed time to cool before stopping.

'Dixie...'

She dropped her hands from the wheel. 'What?'

'I'm sorry I took a shot at your driving.' When she looked she saw that he was smiling slightly. 'You always were a good driver. I should know—I taught you.'

'You shouted at me,' she reminded him. 'On the road to the marina when I had my learner's permit, you shouted at me that I was a fool.' It was one of the few times she'd ever heard his voice raised in anger.

'I thought you were going to kill us both to save that doe.' He rubbed his forehead, and she remembered how his fist had been clenched with anger when her heart had slowed enough for her to see.

The deer had dashed out of the trees in front of the car. Dixie had swerved wildly to avoid hitting the beautiful animal. As the car screamed towards the barrier in a hail of gravel she had known for a terrifying frozen moment that they were going to die, that she had been driving too fast. The car's wild slide had stopped within inches of the barrier between the road and the ocean, and in the silent aftermath Conn's voice had ripped into her.

'You fool! Think first or you'll kill yourself saving the next deer!'

'Do you always think first?' she'd demanded in a trembling voice.

'Damned right I do.'

'You had no right to give me hell over that,' she said softly now. She ran her hand through her short hair. 'That last time you disappeared in Central America they said it was because you stopped to make sure a wounded boy got medical help. You didn't think first then, did you?'

He made a gesture that told her he wouldn't talk about it. Whatever he was willing to say had already been said to a microphone and broadcast to the world.

He opened his door. 'I'll get the food at the hamburger stand. You take Wolf and find us a table.'

Dixie walked through the empty picnic tables and sat down at the one closest to the water. Wolf sprawled at her side on the grass. This was a quiet corner in the city, an almost deserted scrap of parkland on a backwater of the harbour. She watched Connar standing at the burger stand. She knew she was in danger, because her eyes were hungry for the sight of him. It wasn't the same as watching him on television. Here she knew that he might turn at any moment and lock gazes with her.

He came towards her with his hands full of packaged fast food. He spilled it all on to the table and unwrapped one hamburger for Wolf.

'Don't, Conn! I don't feed him junk!'

It was too late. Wolf had possession of the burger and immediately tore it into pieces on the ground.

Connar watched the dog with amusement. 'He has no objection to junk food.'

'No, but you see he was starving when we found him in the market in Ensenada, eating garbage and junk and sleeping in back alleys.' She hugged herself as if the sun overhead had no warmth.

'We?' he asked. 'You and who else?'

His lips had pulled into a straight line, and she felt her heart pounding raggedly as he glared at her. Wolf looked up from the remaining few scraps of hamburger bun and growled low in his throat at Connar.

'Your lover?' suggested Connar.

'You're determined to saddle me with a lover, aren't you?' She shivered, because she hadn't made a mistake earlier. Under the calm surface he was furious. Perhaps he even hated her.

'You haven't denied it,' he reminded her.

If she was smart she wouldn't deny having a lover. If Connar knew she'd been faithful all these years it wouldn't take him long to leap to the next conclusion—that she still loved him. She didn't. Perhaps she was obsessed with the man, but there was no way it was love.

'I was with Sue,' she said. 'She's a neighbour—my landlady actually.' She avoided his eyes so that he wouldn't see the lie. 'We—Sue and I—were in the market, and...he didn't belong to anyone and he was eating garbage. W——I took him home and I promised him he'd never eat like that again, that he'd always have good, nutritious food.' She flushed and looked away, because Connar was watching her with such strange intensity. 'Promises are important to me.'

'All those birthdays,' he said.

She shrugged. 'Yes, I suppose.'

'You always seemed philosophical about it.'

She hugged herself more tightly. 'Nobody should break promises to children or animals.'

He sat down across from her. 'Don't promises to adults matter?'

She could feel her face flaming, and she couldn't find anywhere to look but at Connar. The trees behind him blurred. She heard Wolf noisily devouring the forbidden food and told herself to lean over to look at Wolf... anywhere but at Connar, who was staring at her with a challenge and a question.

'Yes,' she said. 'They matter.'

His hands took possession of one of the paper-wrapped hamburgers. He began to turn it in circles in his grasp. 'Why did you run away? The real reason this time, Dixie.'

There was no way she could tell him how agonisingly she'd loved him when he was glaring at her with a mixture of anger and frustration.

'You married me,' he reminded her. 'We exchanged vows and you gave the marriage twenty-four hours.' He reached one hand across and covered her hand with it. 'Couldn't you have given us more chance than that?'

She shook her head silently.

'When we made love...was that it?' His voice sounded thick and husky. 'You were a virgin. I hadn't expected that, and perhaps I...but I thought you and Jason must have...' She looked up and saw something dark in his eyes. 'Was that why, Dixie? Because of our lovemaking?'

She bit her lip and tried to look away from his eyes, but her gaze was locked into his. His eyes widened slightly as the flush heated her face, and still she couldn't look away.

'At the time,' he said slowly, 'I thought you were enjoying our lovemaking as much as I was.' She tried to pull her hand away from his, but his fingers tightened over hers. 'Dixie...the way I remember it——'

'Damn you!' A shudder swept over her body.

His thumb brushed across the back of her hand. 'Then didn't you owe our marriage more of a chance than you gave it?'

'Stop sounding so bloody reasonable!' She sucked in a breath of air that felt hot and too bulky. 'You were all set to leave me.'

He sat back and she pulled her hand free. She remembered that morning. She would never forget. She had woken alone in the bed where they'd made love. Her mind had been slow with the aftermath of a night of passion. Connar's loving had unleashed frightening needs inside her, had driven her to a trembling fulfillment that left her exposed and vulnerable. She had woken with the echo of his touch on her. While she was lying alone in the bed where he'd taken her innocence—where she'd offered herself to him with her love—one cold fact emerged grimly from the heated storm of passion that had been last night.

Connar didn't love her.

Dixie Bradshaw now belonged body and soul to Connar Stanford. Forever. She'd even told him. She'd said the words 'I love you' and begged him to love her. With the morning sun blazing in on her that

memory terrified her, because she understood now
that whatever he felt for her it wasn't love. He'd told
her how he loved her beauty...her passion...her soft
white skin that responded so wildly to his touch.

But he'd never said that he loved *her*. And if he
was *ever* going to say the words it would have been
last night.

When she heard the telephone ring her mind went
blank for an endless second. The sound came from
downstairs, and as it reached her she knew the future
with a sick certainty. She shot out of Connar's bed
and stood naked in the middle of his room with her
heart pounding. She grabbed the first thing that came
to hand...Connar's white shirt. She slid her arms
into it and ran downstairs with the lapels pulled
together with one hand because she couldn't take the
time to fasten the buttons.

She flew down the stairs with the sick sense of a
nightmare on her, the need to struggle against fate,
and the knowledge that she would lose. The telephone... All her life the telephone had brought news
of loss and disappointment to her.

The rings had stopped. Connar had answered, and
whoever was calling was going to take Connar from
her. Halfway down the stairs the rumble of his voice
shifted into words she could understand.

'Call when you get my flight booked. All I need is
an hour here and I'm ready.'

He was replacing the receiver as she reached the
bottom step. She stood with her hand on the banister
knob, and she could see her fate in his face.

'Get *you* a flight?' she demanded. 'Where?'

She heard the sound of a cow bawling from the next farm . . . smelled coffee that Connar must have brewed only moments ago . . . saw his hand push back the hair from his forehead. He had been awake for some time, had showered and dressed in jeans and a sweatshirt, had been outside—walking, perhaps.

It was as if he'd lived a whole life while she slept.

'Africa,' he said. 'There's been an assassination.'

She gulped and asked painfully, 'What about Paris?' but she already knew that he would leave her. The network had called, and all her life she'd known that she was nothing to the network. She'd created a fantasy life that she would live with Connar. As she stood there dressed only in his silk shirt that dream crumbled around her.

'I have to pack,' he said. His voice was brisk, businesslike.

'Not us?' She knew she shouldn't ask, but couldn't stop herself. Her words seemed slow and thick. 'Just you? You're flying out there to—to Africa alone?'

'That's right.' Already his mind was thousands of miles from her.

'Will I . . .?' She swallowed painfully. 'Do you plan for me to join you?'

She saw his eyes flicker, as if her questions were an irritation. He stepped on to the first stair before he answered, his mind a world away. Someone had been assassinated. She would see it on the news, would watch Connar's life on the news. Yesterday had been a mockery, vows exchanged, but he hadn't taken her as his partner. He'd put his ring on her finger and he was going to leave her behind, the same way she'd been left behind all those years while her father made promises that never came true.

'I'll call,' he said, 'when I get a chance—things are chaotic over there. You'd better go back to Vancouver for the moment.'

Forever. She shuddered and knew she mustn't beg him to love her.

'Connar...take me with you... Please take me with you!'

He touched her shoulder, and she bit her lips and trembled.

'I promised Dev I'd look after you,' he said. 'Taking you into the line of fire is no way to do it.'

'You promised Daddy?' She twisted her wedding-ring on her finger. 'Is that why you married me?'

His thumb rubbed her shoulder gently. 'I don't have time for this, Dixie. Not now.'

She shuddered and knew he would never love her. He had made love to her last night. Of course he had. She had gone to his room dressed for her bridal de-flowering, and of course he'd taken her. He wasn't cruel enough to send her away when she'd actually begged him to make love to her.

There was passion between them, but he had felt passion for other women. She could be anyone. The only reason he'd married her had to be because of that promise. What better way to look after her? It wasn't as if he was giving up the chance of a perfect marriage with some other woman in the future. He'd told her often enough that he intended never to marry because he wanted his freedom. But a few days ago he'd said marrying Dixie was different, and she had told herself he meant because he loved her.

He'd promised to look after her. It was the wildest irony that he had married her to keep a promise to her father—a man who had left a trail of broken promises a mile wide!

She lifted her chin and met his eyes. He was frowning, but she saw the impatience in his eyes, and if there was any hope left it died then.

'Do you want me to pack for you?' she asked stiffly.

'No,' he said. 'I'll do it.'

She sat in the kitchen with a cup of coffee in front of her and his white shirt covering her nakedness, sat with tension and loss building inside as his feet made sounds overhead. Then she got up and climbed the stairs and walked directly into her old childhood room and closed the door. A moment later he knocked lightly.

She hugged herself tightly and stared at the door. She willed him to open it, to come to her. She ached for him to tell her that he didn't want to leave her, that he would yearn for her when he was on the other side of the world. That one day he would learn to love her.

She stared at the door with her heart pounding, and mercifully there was anger welling up. She'd vowed that when she grew up she would never...never... *never* let anyone leave her behind again! She'd always wanted to marry Connar, but that had been a fool's dream. Because she'd imagined that he would love her enough to want to keep her close. She'd never dreamed he could abandon her and walk away without looking back.

'Dixie,' he called through the door, 'I'm going down to Evan's to talk about the farm.'

He must have waited for her to answer, because she heard only silence for a long breath. Then she heard him leaving. He would look after her, of course. He'd promised. There would be money from him and phone calls. And when he had time for her he would come and casually turn her life upside-down. He would share a bed with her on those visits and he'd enjoy her body, because there had been passion last night. But one day she would be so desperate that she'd run after him, screaming and begging. And on that day he would leave, just as he was leaving now.

She dressed in jeans and a cotton blouse. Then she picked up a jacket and her handbag. She put her toothbrush in her bag. Other than the clothes she wore, that was the only thing she took with her— a toothbrush.

'Why did you run?' asked Connar again. Today's Connar, the man who had found her after seven years.

She realised that the fingers of her right hand were clutching her empty ring finger. She spread her hands flat on the table and stared at her short, plainly polished nails. 'Because I understood how it was going to be. You weren't going to send for me.' She shook her hair back and knew this would be a new nightmare. There was something so sterile about sitting in a beautiful park with a table between them while they dissected a marriage that had never really existed. 'You married me and walked away—flew away.'

'I didn't have time for explanations.' He pulled the wrapper off one of the hamburgers and stared at the bun. 'You must have understood that.'

She picked up the discarded paper and crumpled it in one hand. 'What I understood was that being married to you meant putting my life on hold while you lived yours! I came second to every fool in the world with a gun or a cause!' She dragged in a hungry breath and heard the echo of her own rising voice. 'I couldn't do it—waiting...wondering...never knowing if you even thought of me when you were off risking your life in the cause of news.'

She strained to hear Connar's breathing and heard nothing. Wolf's panting came loudly over the sound of traffic on the freeway near by.

'You knew what it would be like before you married me.'

'I was young and stupid and I thought...' She spread her hands helplessly, and the crumpled paper she'd forgotten went tumbling silently down on to the grass. 'You shouldn't have married me when you didn't want me with you!'

'I'd have sent for you. When I got back to Paris.'

'Would you?' Perhaps he would have. She sighed and said quietly, 'Unless there was some other emergency, some other political situation where a wife wasn't convenient. And what would happen after Paris?'

He pushed back from the bench. 'You're right,' he said.

She stood when he did. Wolf scrambled to his feet too.

'I loved you then,' she said in a low voice. 'I was insanely in love with you. That's the real reason I left. Because I was fool enough when I married you to think it meant you felt the same.'

'Dixie——'

'I know! You don't believe in that kind of love.'
She forced a smile. 'But I did when I married you. If
I'd stayed I would have spent my life waiting and I'd
have turned into a bitter woman, because back then
I believed.'

Long heartbeats of silence. Dixie bent down to
scratch Wolf's ear.

'So you left me. And you're a success now instead
of a bitter woman?' His eyes were dark, shadowed
from the sun by the big tree beside them. She couldn't
tell what he was really feeling. 'You've changed,' he
said. 'You're more sure of yourself.'

She managed another smile. 'Not a child any more?'

'I had no business marrying you then.' His face was
as harsh as his voice. 'Your father hardly buried and
Jason sniffing around you—he wanted you back. I
suppose I should have let him have a chance.' He ran
both hands through his unruly hair, and she had the
feeling again that he was deliberately hanging on to
that cool exterior to cover some strong emotion.

'You'd promised my father you'd look after me,'
she reminded him.

'That was part of it, of course.' His smile was grim.
'But part of it was me.' He moved abruptly, and Wolf
turned and growled at him. 'I wanted you,' he said
flatly. 'And if I'd left you, then you'd have ended up
with Jason.'

Her hand froze in Wolf's fur. 'You wanted me?
Sexually?'

He shrugged and she felt dizzy, because he must
have desired her strongly to go to the extent of marrying her. She'd believed that the explosion of passion

between them had been only a matter of one night for him. It had been more than that. He would never have loved her the way she needed, but she might have stayed if she'd known, might have slowly broken her heart beating her love against his desire.

'The time was all wrong,' he said. 'But we were friends already and I thought we could make a go of it.' He reached out as if he would touch her, but something in her face must have stopped him. 'I didn't know you thought you were in love with me until our wedding night, when you . . . I did know you were attracted, though, and I thought that given time——'

'Time? How much time have you spent on this continent since I left you?'

'A few months this year.'

'And the other years?'

He grimaced. 'A week here and there.'

'That's not enough to sustain even the pale shadow of a marriage. Why didn't you just seduce me? I'd have . . .' Her face flamed, and suddenly the tension was strong between them. She felt her lips part, and his eyes responded as if she were inviting his kiss and he were about to give her what she needed.

'I promised Dev I'd look after you,' he said simply.

'You couldn't square seducing me with your conscience?'

'A mistake,' he agreed. 'One I've regretted. I never intended to hurt you.'

'Well——' she managed to put a casual tone into her words '—it doesn't matter now. I got over it. So . . .' She drew in a deep breath. 'So where do we go from here?'

'Let's walk,' he said, gesturing towards the trees to her left.

She knew what was next. She had to tell him about Jess.

His anger had gone quiet, as if he had lost the need to fight with her, to conquer her in some way. Maybe this was all he'd wanted on Saturday night: a quiet talk; her real reasons for running.

'You've lived in Mexico all this time?' he asked. He walked towards the trees where a shallow stream ran. Wolf prowled restlessly at Connar's side.

'How did you figure out about Mexico?'

'Your pictures. The market scene. That girl playing on the beach. It had a Latin-American feel to it.'

If anyone could recognise a Latin-American atmosphere it would be Connar. He'd been a terrorist's captive in Central America. He'd reported everything from world conferences to political scandals in South America.

'Your work is good,' he said, 'very good, but of course you know that.'

'You didn't expect me to be good?'

'Not that good.' He turned towards her with a slight smile curving his lips. 'Are you doing all right? If you need money——'

'You don't need to look after me, Conn.'

His eyes searched hers as if he didn't quite believe her. Wolf growled, and Connar put his hand on the dog's head. The mongrel abruptly sat down. 'Who is the girl in the portrait I bought?'

In front of them the stream was rippling over rocks on its way to the ocean. She hadn't been able to hear it from the picnic table. She walked to its edge and sat down cross-legged on the grass. She realised that she hadn't the courage to tell him about Jess.

'You have a magic touch with Wolf,' she said.

Connar had always been good with animals. When Aunt Jessie had boarded horses it was Conn who schooled them. When a stray dog had turned up at the farm with a mouthful of painful porcupine quills it was Connar who carefully removed each one while he spoke to the dog in a firm, reassuring voice.

'The picture?' he asked again. 'The girl in the picture.'

She turned her head to look at him, and when she met his eyes she knew he hadn't guessed about Jess. Not yet, but his newsman's instinct told him the picture was something he should probe.

He sat down on the grass a few feet away from her. Wolf lifted his head, but Connar said a word and the mongrel sank back on to the grass.

He touched her shoulder briefly. 'There's something I want to talk about, Dixie.'

'OK,' she agreed, although she knew there would never be a better time to tell him about Jess. He was sitting beside her, and as she watched him he sprawled back on the grass with that relaxed tension that was so familiar to her. No anger in his eyes now. Almost as if they were friends again.

A rock in the middle of the stream was impeding the flow of water. Froth piled up around it, forming a ridge that stood still amid the rushing clear water. Connar's silence stretched into moments, and she remembered other times when they'd sat together at the water's edge and she'd felt lazy contentment.

NO COST! NO OBLIGATION TO BUY!
NO PURCHASE NECESSARY!

PLAY "LUCKY 7"
AND GET AS MANY AS SIX FREE GIFTS...

HOW TO PLAY:

1 With a coin, carefully scratch away the silver panel opposite. You will now be eligible to receive two or more FREE books, and possibly other gifts, depending on what is revealed beneath the scratch off area.

2 When you return this card, you'll receive specially selected **Mills & Boon romances**. We'll send you the books and gifts you qualify for absolutely FREE, and at the same time we'll reserve you a subscription to our Reader Service.

3 If we don't hear from you, within 10 days we'll send you six brand new romances to read and enjoy every month for just £1.90 each, the same price as the books in the shops. There is no extra charge for postage and handling. There are no hidden extras.

4 When you join the Mills & Boon Reader Service, you'll also get our FREE monthly Newsletter, featuring author news, horoscopes, penfriends, competitions.

5 You are under no obligation, and may cancel or suspend your subscription at any time simply by writing to us.

**You'll love your
cuddly teddy.
His brown eyes and
cute face are sure to
make you smile.**

Play "Lucky 7"

Just scratch away the silver panel with a coin.
Then check below to see which gifts you get.

YES! I have scratched away the silver panel. Please send me all the gifts for which I qualify. I understand that I am under no obligation to purchase any books, as explained on the opposite page. I am over 18 years of age.

MS/MRS/MISS/MR   11A4R

ADDRESS

POSTCODE   SIGNATURE

WORTH FOUR FREE BOOKS
PLUS A CUDDLY TEDDY AND MYSTERY GIFT

WORTH FOUR FREE BOOKS
PLUS A MYSTERY GIFT

WORTH FOUR FREE BOOKS

WORTH TWO FREE BOOKS

MILLS & BOON 'NO RISK' GUARANTEE

- You're not required to buy a single book!
- You must be completely satisfied or you may cancel at any time simply by writing to us. You will receive no more books; you'll have no further obligation.
- The free books and gifts you receive from this offer remain yours to keep no matter what you decide.

Mills & Boon Reader Service
FREEPOST
P.O. Box 236
Croydon
Surrey
CR9 9EL

NO
STAMP
NEEDED

'Maybe I've played with death once too often,' he said finally. His voice seemed to come to her from a long way away.

He was toying with a blade of grass on the ground. He twisted it between his fingers and seemed to be studying it intently. 'This last time—in Central America—I promised myself that if I got home I'd have some of the things I've realised I want in my life.'

She tried to look away from him, but her eyes wouldn't obey her mind's command. The lines of his face were deep and hard. Even with the deep seriousness of his words there was something in his eyes that she recognised, as if Connar was mildly amused by life and his own part in it.

'What things?' she asked.

He smoothed the grass in a way that reminded her of his hands on her naked flesh. She shuddered and gripped her waist with arms wrapped tight to shut off the memory.

'Family,' he said. 'A real home.'

'You'd go nuts sitting in one place.'

He smiled. 'Yes, I suppose I would. And I doubt if I could stop trying to dig secrets out of people who have no right to keep them any more than you could stop creating beautiful pictures.' He sat up and leaned his weight on one arm. 'I want a family. New roots. Children. That's why I had to see you. To settle this thing between us.'

She swallowed. 'Settle?'

He leaned across and captured her chin in his hand. 'We can end this marriage, Dix—or else be truly married.'

'Us?'

'Yes. Us.' His voice was sober. No laughter in his eyes. No passion. None of the deep desperation she felt when she thought about the rest of her life without the love she'd once yearned for.

Love and babies and a home. It was too easy to see it, but it was fantasy, because he'd never talked of love and he was a stranger to her now. Perhaps he'd always been a stranger.

'The objective is to have a family?' she asked. 'So if I'm not the woman,' she said grimly, 'then you'll find someone else?'

'We're already married, Dix. I've never cared for the idea of divorce.'

'Because we happen to be married already you want——'

'To try again. Yes.' He pulled a piece of grass out of the ground with a rough motion. 'Is there any reason why we shouldn't? Are you involved with another man?'

She spread one hand out on her thigh and stared at it. It was the hand that had briefly worn his ring. 'Aren't you . . . involved?'

'No.'

Damn Connar! He'd always been able to confuse her. She dug her fingers into the flesh of her thigh and muttered, 'We can't. I won't!'

Thank God she was stronger than she had been seven years ago! 'I think it would be best we get married', he'd said, and it had sent her tumbling into the biggest mistake of her life.

'Of course we can.' His voice was so casual, as if they were discussing politics or the weather. 'You say you won't. Why not?'

'Because...' This was insane! Why hadn't he divorced her for desertion years ago? 'If I ever marry anyone again——'

'We are married, Dixie.' He brushed the grass off his hands.

'Not in any real sense. We never were.' She saw his eyes on her arms and wondered if he could read her response to him from signs in her body. She shook her head sharply. 'No, Connar. I'm not living with any man unless we're in love with each other. There's no other reason that makes it worth while.'

'You were in love with me once.'

She smiled bitterly. 'You don't even believe in love.'

His eyes locked on hers. 'Perhaps not, but whatever you did feel you could feel it again.' She couldn't read anything from his eyes. He was thinking, evaluating, studying her. 'I think we could discuss it,' he said. 'What's to lose in simply talking?'

'No! Absolutely not. Not in a million years.' She made her voice flat and calm, because it was essential to persuade him that she meant this. 'If I fall in love again it will be with a very different sort of man. A man who believes in love.'

She saw something in his eyes, as if he could read more than she meant to tell him. She said desperately, 'I want my freedom, Conn. You scare me. You're a world-class negotiator and you can talk rings around me. So would you please just—divorce me. You're not in love with me. I'm not...' She clenched her hands in on themselves. Aunt Jessie would hate this,

Connar and Dixie trying marriage for twenty-four hours and then tearing it apart in a park in San Diego as if they were discussing dividing up a pie neither wanted. 'I don't love you any more.'

He leaned across and grasped her hand. He spread her fingers the way he had when he'd slipped his ring on to her hand. 'Love is just a word. What's between us isn't over, Dixie.'

He was close beside her. Too close. She could feel his breath on her face. His hand slid over her back, and she knew he was going to kiss her. His mouth drew closer and she told herself to run, to scramble up and away from him. His eyes told her he remembered what had happened when he touched her on their wedding night, that he remembered sliding the lace away and her body responding.

His lips touched hers, and Wolf growled. Connar made a sound low in his throat, as if he were growling back at Wolf. Then he took her into his arms and she was liquid lying against him, telling herself to push away, but his mouth brushed hers and he was murmuring words against her lips.

'You don't know unless you try,' he murmured. His hands found the shape of her back and he made a soft sound that shivered down her spine. She could feel herself answering and she was lost, would be lost again, and this time she would beg for the things he could never give her: to be first in his heart and his love forever.

'Connar...'

'You haven't forgotten,' he murmured. 'Nothing's changed.' He drew his mouth back from hers. He watched her face through heavy-lidded eyes and she

knew he saw her lips trying to follow his to bring him
back—her body voting without permission from her
mind. 'You'll come back to me,' he said. 'You want
this as much as I do.'

His mouth came towards her again, and she felt the
air go out of her lungs in a long stream. 'Connar,
stop! I . . .'

He paused with his lips a heartbeat away from hers.
He touched her mouth with his fingers and traced the
shape of her lips. 'Is that really what you want? Do
you want me to stop? To leave you alone?' His fingers
touched the slight parting of her lips and coaxed a
caress from her mouth, then his mouth moved to take
hers, and she knew she had no strength to pull away.

'There's a child,' she said desperately. 'Your child.'

She felt his arms go rigid. Then he released her, and
she thought for a moment she would tumble to the
grass.

'The girl in the picture?'

She swallowed. 'Yes.'

'When I first saw that picture she reminded me of
you.' He was staring at Wolf, his mouth a hard line
and his voice the neutral sound she'd heard him use
to report tragedy on television. 'You as a little girl.
And for just a moment I thought . . . I wondered . . .'
He shook his head sharply. 'I told myself you wouldn't
keep that from me. Not for six years. She'd have to
be six years old?'

She swallowed. 'Next month.'

He stood abruptly. 'I want to see her. I want to see
her *now*.'

'Yes,' she said, but she knew it would not end there.
Connar was accustomed to taking control, and this

would be no different. 'We live about fifteen miles across the border,' she said. 'You'd better bring your own car. I'll take you to pick it up.'

'No. You can drive me.'

She knew danger when she saw it. Connar's eyes were hard and his face was all deep lines.

'I don't want to drive back to San Diego tonight and you'll need——'

'You can put me up overnight. I am your daughter's father.' He smiled grimly. 'And *your* husband.'

'No,' she said.

'We don't even have a legal separation.' He pinned her with cold blue eyes. 'If you want a fight, Dixie, I'm in the mood. We can paint the courts red. Or you can give a little.'

'Give what?' Herself at the altar of a love that would never be returned? She didn't love him! It had been a child's fantasy, and she'd been stupid enough at twenty to think it could come true.

Fairy-tales.

'Whether you like it or not,' he declared grimly, 'things are going to change now.'

CHAPTER SIX

THE Mexican guard at the border waved them through without even a question.

'Shouldn't I have a tourist visa?' asked Connar.

She geared up and around a sharp curve that seemed to be banked in reverse. 'You can stay three days without formality if you don't go beyond Ensenada.'

'And you don't live past Ensenada?'

'No.'

They drove for a mile in silence. With each breath Dixie took she was aware of the faint scent of Connar's aftershave. He was too real, too close, sitting beside her in a knit shirt that did nothing to hide the strength of his arms or the breadth of his chest. When the signposting for the toll highway came, Dixie turned off on to the free coastal road. She normally took the toll road, but today she welcomed driving through the villages. She needed the distraction of the policeman standing in the middle of a village street, stopping traffic and soliciting donations for the local hospital. Dixie handed over a two-thousand-peso note and Connar put in ten American dollars.

'I thought you'd be immune to that sort of thing,' she said as she drove away from the policeman. She felt ashamed as she spoke, because she knew better. Connar cared. He always had.

'I doubt you thought at all,' he said grimly. He was leaning back in the seat, and he'd undone the top two buttons of his shirt. 'Do you live in one of these expatriate cliff-hanging houses?'

They had been passing a number of American-style houses between the villages, modern structures perched on the cliffs looking out to the Pacific Ocean.

'Something like that,' Dixie agreed. 'I rent a small guest cottage from an American woman who owns one of those cliff-hangers.'

'When exactly did you come down here?'

She shrugged. She didn't know why she didn't simply tell him what he wanted to know. He'd get it out of her in the end.

'After you had the baby?' he asked with his newsman's voice.

'Before.' She sighed. 'Just before Jess was born.'

'You named her for my mother?'

'She was a mother to me, too.' She felt tears welling up, and blinked repeatedly to defeat them. She kept her eyes on the road, but she could feel that Connar was watching her.

'Stop the van.'

She pulled up in the middle of the road. In the States someone would be honking, but this was Mexico. The car behind simply swerved out and drove around them. From the side of the road someone called out in Spanish.

'How is her birth registered?'

'Here,' she said on a whisper. 'Here in Mexico.'

'And the father?' His voice went hard and bleak. 'If you tell me that you put "father unknown" I—I think I'll throttle you!'

'Of course I didn't!' She bit her lip painfully. 'I wouldn't——'

'You wouldn't keep her from me?' he suggested softly. 'But that's what you did, isn't it?'

'I know it was wrong.' She spread her fingers out on the steering-wheel, then clenched them again. 'But when I found out I was pregnant I could hardly come back and say I'd changed my mind because I was having a baby. I did plan to tell you. Afterwards.'

'How long did you plan to wait?' His lips twisted. 'Until she was ten? Fifteen? Perhaps in time for her twenty-first birthday?'

She shook her head blindly and fought tears that wanted to overflow. 'You were in the Middle East after she was born. I watched and I thought when you came back I'd... Then you disappeared in Lebanon. I thought you were dead—everybody thought—and I watched every day, terrified they'd show you being killed.' Her voice was brittle. 'And I thought about her watching—the way I did when the terrorists shot my father—and Jess...' She made a sound between a whimper and a sob. 'I wanted her to be happy. Not dreaming about visits from a daddy who spent her life calling to cancel.'

His hand closed into a fist against his thigh. 'You tarred me with your father's brush without even a trial.' He closed his eyes and muttered, 'What a bloody mess!'

She curled her fingers around the steering-wheel. 'My father was your mentor. You thought the world of him.'

'Children see adults in black and white,' he said without inflexion. 'By the time I started following in Dev's footsteps I wasn't blind to his faults.' He smiled wryly. 'I admired him, yes. Professionally. And I liked him—he was a likeable man. But I'd happily have strangled him for the way he made promises to you when he had to know he couldn't keep them. Do you imagine that just because we followed the same profession your father and I have the same idea of how to be parents?'

'That would be terrible stereotyping, wouldn't it?' she whispered. She'd reacted, assumed. She'd even run from him, based on an assumption locked into her mind in the instant the telephone had rung that morning. Perhaps the unforgivable thing was that in seven years she hadn't really questioned that assumption when it came to Jess.

'If you really believed that... Oh, hell, Dixie!'

'I didn't want Jess hurt,' she said.

'Does she know about me?'

'Yes. She asked and I... She watches for you on television.'

'So you didn't protect her from that after all.' He smiled wryly. 'And how did you explain my failure to have anything to do with her? Did you tell her I didn't give a damn? Did you——?'

She shook her head wildly. 'No! No, Conn. I told her you didn't know. That we'd separated and I never told you there was a child. I said one day we'd write to you and you'd...' She blinked, and it was no use at all, because the tears overflowed.

He gripped her arm and she winced. 'Get out. I'll drive.'

She opened the door and slid out, walked around the front of the van. They passed each other at the left front bumper. He stopped and took her shoulders in his hands and stared down at her.

'Thank you for telling her the truth,' he said soberly.

'I wouldn't have——'

'Lied? I guess I knew that. Stop worrying, Dix. It'll work out.'

She didn't see how. A minute ago he'd said it was a mess, and he'd been right. Jess was going to love her daddy on sight, and Connar would want more than visiting rights. He would want control and involvement. She should have realised from the beginning that Connar would never be the sort of father Devlin Bradshaw had been. Her own father had cared about her only when it was convenient. She'd come second, third, sometimes even last in his priorities. But Connar...events in South America or Africa might weigh above his own family, but he wouldn't make promises he couldn't keep.

Except for that one time—the vows he'd made when they married. And maybe that was why she'd believed so easily that letting Jess know Connar could be a disaster. Or perhaps she had only pretended to believe because it was so much easier than dealing with how to share Jess with Connar and keep her own heart intact. She didn't love him any more, but the chemistry was still there. Dangerous chemistry.

Connar shifted the van into gear and started smoothly into motion. Considering that the clutch was badly in need of replacement, she didn't know how he managed to drive slowly through the village without the slightest lurch.

'I might have known this would end up with you at the wheel,' she muttered.

'You never did like compromises,' he said drily. 'That's why we're in this mess.'

'When did you ever offer a compromise?'

He gave her a sharp glance as he braked for a trio of young boys kicking an old soccer ball across the dusty street. 'When did I force you into anything?' he countered. 'If we're going to argue old grievances, be specific.'

She made a frustrated sound. He hadn't forced her to marry him, hadn't forced her home when she'd run away to Vancouver on her fifteenth birthday. Both times he'd handled her with words, and she'd followed blindly in the direction he'd pointed.

'Are we going to argue?' he asked, and she recognised the tone in his voice from other times when her anger had butted against his logic.

She drew her legs up and circled her knees with her arms. 'There's no point arguing with you. You make everything into a damned debate.'

'There's nothing wrong with a bit of logic.'

She flushed at the amusement in his voice. She turned her head and stared through the windscreen to the right, so that she couldn't see him even in her peripheral vision. She concentrated hard on the scene ahead: a dusty street; Mexican children playing barefoot; a warm day moving towards hot. If she could set her easel up right over there she could catch the essence of lazy, innocent warmth in a few strokes.

'You use logic like a weapon,' she said slowly. 'Maybe that's why I'm scared to let you into Jess's life.'

'What do you imagine I'll do to her?'

'You'll try to take over.' She hugged her knees tighter and stared through the windscreen. 'You'll decide how her life should be on your own. What I feel or want—none of that will matter.' She looked at him. He was looking straight ahead, driving with a relaxed ease that angered her. 'I won't let you take over, Conn. I'm not a child any more and I'm not living in your shadow. She's my daughter and——'

'Aren't you borrowing trouble? Why don't you wait for the problems before you fight the battle?'

She sucked in an angry breath. 'I'm just letting you know—giving you warning. Jess lives with me. She's always... She's in my custody.' She saw from the sudden deep line that appeared beside his mouth that she'd made a mistake.

'Are you saying that's how you want to deal with this situation?' He was watching the road ahead, but his face was grim. 'A custody battle? Which way do I turn here?'

'Conn, I didn't——'

'Which way?'

'Right.'

He jerked on the wheel and the van lurched into the right lane. 'Do you want to settle this in court?'

She had a vision of herself in the witness box and Connar cross-examining her. She told herself it wouldn't be like that. It would be a lawyer, not Connar. But he would hire someone like himself, a shark who could use words like a sword. And she wouldn't look good on the stand. People were always telling her she looked seventeen, not ten years older. In court he could paint her as an immature child who'd married and run, as a child who had selfishly kept her daughter a secret, sneaking across the border into a foreign country. He could make her look irresponsible. Immature. Perhaps even unfit as a mother.

'Would you?' she whispered. 'Would you take me to court?'

He didn't answer.

Both the house and the cottage were empty when Connar and Dixie arrived.

'Jess and Sue were going to the market,' explained Dixie.

'Sue?' he asked, his brows lifted in a question that reminded her of how little he knew of her life these last seven years. 'Your landlady? And she's also the friend who was with you when you found Wolf?'

She bit her lip. 'It was Jess with me. I... Sue... I rent the cottage from her.' She gestured to the small, whitewashed Mediterranean-style guest house that was just visible beyond the house. 'That's my place. I guess we could wait inside.'

But once inside he was restless, prowling and studying the sketches and portraits on her walls, striding from the market scenes to the painting she'd done of Jess and Wolf running together over the rocks.

'She has your colouring,' he said.

She wanted to ask him what was going to happen next. She knew her life would change, knew that somehow she must walk this tightrope. He would try to take control, and she would have to fight him. The prospect made her feel nauseous.

'She has your eyes, Conn.'

He turned back from the picture. 'How did you manage when you found you were pregnant? I used to wonder how on earth you were surviving.' His mouth thinned into a straight line, and she saw anger under the civilised exterior.

She met his gaze squarely. 'Does that make us even, then?' she asked. 'Because I've wondered often enough what terrible thing would happen to you next.'

He brushed that aside with a gesture. 'There was money from your father's insurance policy. It's still there. And I... You could at least have asked me for money.'

'I wasn't helpless!' She bit her lip on the hostility she heard in her own voice. 'Did you think I couldn't look after myself? I was working as a chambermaid when I realised I was pregnant and——'

'A chambermaid? Couldn't you have found something in an art gallery?'

'I was afraid you'd find me.'

Connar stepped towards her. She shivered and jerked back as if he'd actually touched her.

'I knew you'd look for me. That's where you would have looked. Art galleries. Art schools.'

He stopped abruptly and jammed his hands into his pockets. 'Would it have been so terrible if I'd found you?'

'Would you have let me go my own way?'

He glared at her. 'You worked as a chambermaid while you carried my child. Surely you knew that I would have looked after you?' A muscle jerked in his jaw. 'Even if you found it so impossible to live with me.'

'Live *with* you?' She managed to speak softly, but the rage boiled through. 'I'd be stashed away on Thetis Island while you bopped around with a microphone, taking the temperature of the world, leaving *me* to watch from the sidelines! And I'd have . . .' The anger drained out of her. 'Can't we stop dissecting the past? The marriage is over.' She reached out one hand, then jerked it back when she touched his shoulder and felt a muscle flex under her fingers.

'It's never going to be over,' he said softly. He pinned her with his eyes. 'Not now.' He took his hands out of his pockets and touched her shoulders, turning her around to face the wall and Jess's portrait. She could see the window too, and through it the flash of red that was Sue's car pulling up outside.

'We made this child together,' he said in a low voice. 'Whatever else there is between us, she makes it impossible for us to be separate from each other.'

She knew he was right. He would be on the television, his name tumbling off Jess's quick tongue and—God help her—haunting her with every beat of her heart!

She *should* have made herself date more, forced herself to find a man who could make her forget Connar, a man who could erase his voice from her memory, wash away the dream of his body, hard and hot and agonisingly wonderful against hers.

His fingers moved lightly over her shoulders. She felt their pressure shift as she took each breath. There was nowhere to move away. The wall of pictures was in front of her and Connar behind.

'I met Sue at the hotel where I was working,' she said, talking quickly to wipe out the sensation of his thumb moving on her flesh. Did he know he was caressing her? Or was it automatic, an unconscious motion of thumbs and fingers?

Had it been automatic that night when he had pushed the satin and lace away and carried her to his bed, turned the lights dim, and bent down over her mouth as he'd begun to caress her body? No. He said he had wanted her when he married her, that he desired her sexually.

Stop it!

'In San Diego,' she muttered raggedly. She heard a car door slam outside.

'San Diego?' he urged when her silence stretched too long.

She moved restlessly. 'I had just found out that I... Sue's husband had just died and she didn't know what to do. She'd been injured in the accident that killed him and...' She was talking faster and faster, the words tumbling. 'She... well... couldn't live alone down here. She'd just got out of hospital and was staying in the hotel. But she... she wanted to... she said they'd been happy here and... We talked. I was cleaning her room one day and she...'

Sue had come in with tears dried on her face and her lips pressed thin with pain. That was when it had started, the talking, the friendship. Dixie turned around abruptly, and it was worse facing him with the wall behind her. His hands were still on her...lightly curved around her upper arms. His chest was only inches away, his eyes watching her as if the questions were in his eyes and not on his voice. She could see a small white scar just below his right eye. It didn't show when he was on television.

'And?' he asked. His lips seemed harder than she remembered. The muscles around his jaw were more rigid. The lines were deeper on his face. But his hair was still that unruly dark blond and she could see no touch of grey.

'Sue needed someone to live with her, to help her— she . . . and I needed——'

'A place to have our child?'

'Yes.' She heard something else slam outside. The boot of the car. 'It worked for both of us,' she said. She knew she should pull away from his touch, go outside and shove Sue and Jess between herself and Connar. He was watching her as if he was remembering that night. As if he was wondering what would happen if his hands moved down her arms and captured her hands and brought them to his face.

If he brought her close and melded her body into his, his mouth to hers, his hard thighs against her softness . . .

She shuddered and tried to pull back, but the wall was against her and Connar close in front of her. His hands flattened as he moved his palms down towards her elbows.

'Conn,' she breathed. His pupils widened and she gulped. 'After Jess was born I—I stayed because Sue needed me still and it gave me a way of looking after Jess until I could make enough money from selling my work. I . . . Then later when Sue didn't need help so much I—I rented this guest house from her. We...' Footsteps on the flagstones outside. Jess's light, quick tread. Sue's slower walk and the sound of the cane making her gait rhythmically uneven. 'They're back,' she breathed.

Connar didn't step back, and she knew she couldn't breathe until he did. If her breathing brought them into contact . . . She was so tangled in the scent of him and the memories from his touch. It was insane, but the old memories were stronger than the sounds around her, the old hunger new and unbelievably strong.

It *wasn't* what she wanted! She would burn up in his arms. Then afterwards... Never again! Never, *never* again!

The door opened.

Connar's head turned. She saw his body freeze. Jess was in the doorway. Sue came up behind Jess, her long, fiery hair contrasting with Jess's short dark waves.

Jess—brown hair, tanned bare legs dark against the white of her shorts and T-shirt. Jess...for once frozen in place. She stared at Connar and he stared back. Two sets of probing blue eyes assessing each other.

'You're my daddy,' she said finally. 'Aren't you?' She planted one small hand on her straight hip. Her small mouth frowned, as if she were measuring Connar and might reject him for the role of father if he failed her test. 'You're tidier on television,' she said.

Connar took one step towards Jess, only one. Jess's eyes widened, but she didn't back up. Behind Jess, Sue lifted a silent hand in a gesture that acknowledged Dixie.

'Yes,' Connar said. 'I am your father.'

She saw in his face the determination to form a bond with this child. Then she looked at Jess and saw what Connar saw. Dark hair and tanned skin. Brilliant blue eyes that would not be ignored. A deep, small voice that seemed too old for its owner. A way of watching as she spoke as if she could read the very air the words were carried on.

Connar's daughter.

'Why are you never on television any more?' demanded Jess.

'It's only been a month,' said Dixie. She bit her lip when Connar's eyes swept to her face. She felt the flush crawling along her throat. He'd always been able to read her secrets, and now he would know that she watched him always.

'I'm here instead,' he told Jess. He watched, as if judging what impact his words had on her. 'I would have come sooner if I'd known about you. I would have come right away.'

Jess nodded soberly. 'My mom said you would.'

'What have you been doing today?' he asked, watching Jess carefully, as if reading her body language, evaluating her responses before he made any move towards her. She'd been afraid that Connar would expect instant affection from Jess, but he was wiser than that.

Jess came one step into the room, one step closer to Connar, but she stopped out of his reach. 'We went to the beach. There was a man with sunburn like my Barbie's red coat.' She grimaced, as if with sympathetic pain for the man's burn. 'And Maria had her birthday. She's six and we ate burritos, but Maria couldn't eat six even though she tried.'

'Is Maria your best friend?'

'Hmm.' Jess frowned. 'Maybe. But we argue sometimes. I'm teaching Maria English. She can't talk like us cos she's Mexican and her mom and dad don't know English.'

'*Hablé español*?'

'*Sí*,' she agreed soberly. 'Do you want to see my Barbie dolls?'

'If you'll show them to me.'

She nodded, looking small and serious, a slight smile glowing in her eyes. 'Come on, then,' she offered, and she turned and hurried towards the corridor that led to her room.

Connar followed her out of the room.

Dixie met Sue's eyes, and it was a moment before either of them spoke. Sue stepped inside and looked around the living-room, as if she thought there might be signs of a fight between Connar and Dixie.

'Are you OK?' Sue asked.

Dixie nodded. 'Yes—I don't know. Ever since I told him he's been pretty reasonable, but I know he's angry.'

'Well . . .' Sue looked towards the corridor. They could hear sounds: Connar's low voice asking questions; Jess answering, her voice quickening with enthusiasm.

Dixie voiced the thought in Sue's eyes. 'He has a right to be angry.'

'Do you want to entertain him here for dinner?' Sue asked. 'Or do you want to eat at the house so I can thin out the atmosphere?'

'Please! I'll go mad if. . . I guess he's staying. I don't know where I can put him.'

'In your bed,' suggested Sue. 'You are still married to the man.'

'No,' she whispered. 'Definitely not in *my* bed! Jess can sleep with me and I'll let him have her room.'

'He can stay at my house,' suggested Sue, 'but don't keep him out of your bed just for the principle of the thing. You'll regret it if you do.'

It should have been a deeply tense afternoon and evening, because Dixie knew exactly what Connar was doing. She didn't talk much herself. Mostly she watched Connar, and he didn't talk a lot either, but every word counted. He helped Jess bathe Wolf, a job that soaked them both and had Jess screaming with laughter. Jess was chattering and spilling out the details of their life, telling Connar how they spent their days and who their friends were.

'Alex?' he asked when the name came tumbling out of Jess's mouth. 'Who's Alex?'

'Our friend,' said Jess. 'He's grown up. He lives in Ens'nada. Wolf, you be still!'

Conn put one hand on Wolf's head and scratched behind the dog's soapy ear. 'What does Alex do?'

'Stuff,' said Jess vaguely. 'He takes mom dancing.'

Dixie turned away to reach for a towel for Wolf. She knew Connar was watching her. He wanted to read her eyes to know about Alex, and she wasn't going to let him. She couldn't remember the feel of Alex's arms any more than she could remember what it had felt like when she was at art college and trying to be in love with Jason.

Over dinner Connar drew Sue out. It was the first time Dixie had heard Sue talk without tension about how she and her husband had bought this house on their honeymoon, how they'd talked about retiring here one day. Sue's voice was a little sad, but Dixie realised that in the last few years Sue's grief had eased so that she could talk about the past and remember the good parts without losing herself in the pain of losing Brett.

'When I lost my husband,' she told Connar, 'this seemed a good place to come. Somehow it was easier here. Maybe for a while I pretended that the dream had come true, that we'd retired here and he was just out for a walk.'

People talked to Connar. It wasn't really the words he said, because he was often silent. It was simply that he had a magic that made people want to confide in him, some magic that had Jess reaching for his hand as if she'd been running at his side holding his hand since she was a toddler, that let Sue talk as if he were an old friend she could tell anything to.

Connar was interested in everyone, but Dixie told herself she had better not forget how easily he'd been willing to walk away from her only a day after they married. She'd promised herself when she'd run from him that she would never be anyone's left-over again. She'd made that promise to herself when she was a girl, but she'd broken it when she married Connar. Left behind, waiting, not living her life, because her heart was on the other side of the world.

Better to be alone. Better to have her own life than be sucked into living and breathing for the next time Connar looked her way.

'I want you to tuck me in,' demanded Jess at bedtime.

Dixie felt tears burning behind her eyes.

Connar stared at Jess as if he could read her thoughts, then he said, 'Your mom and I both will.' He reached out his hand for Dixie.

She knew it was a mistake to take his hand, to walk hand in hand following Jess into her room, Jess wearing that silly nightgown with a big picture of a kangaroo on it and Connar's warm fingers sending shivers all the way up Dixie's arm. She bent down to kiss Jess goodnight and then she tried to leave, but Connar held her hand tightly.

'Will you be here tomorrow?' Jess asked Connar. Dixie marvelled that she was able to ask the question with her eyes wide and trusting. She remembered her own childhood, knowing that the answers her father gave were mostly not dependable, and afraid to ask because she was afraid of being disappointed.

'Tomorrow I'm going back to San Diego,' Connar said. He touched the top of her head and smoothed the dark short hair. 'If you and your mom pack a suitcase I'll come back the next day and we'll go to my place up in Canada.'

Jess had been lying down with her head nestled in the pillow, but Conn's words made her jerk to a sitting position. 'The island?' she demanded. 'The island you told me about? I always wanted to be on an island!'

Dixie jerked her hand, but Connar wouldn't let her go. He bent down and kissed Jess goodnight, then said, 'Come on,' to Dixie, and she had no choice but to walk out of Jess's room with him, because he had her hand trapped firmly until they got to the living-room. Then she jerked and she was free and gasping, as if it had been a rough physical battle between them.

'Come outside!' she hissed.

She stormed out of the front door, aware of Connar behind her, of her own pulsing anger and how it contrasted to what she saw when she looked at his face.

She swung around to face him when she got to the edge of the cliff.

'Are you planning to jump over?' he asked.

'Don't ever do that again! Don't use Jess against me!'

A pause, a heartbeat. He tilted his head slightly and watched her through narrowed eyes, as if she amused him. 'What exactly did I do?'

'You invited Jess to your place!'

He pushed one hand through his hair. It curled wildly at the touch of his fingers. 'And there's some reason I shouldn't?'

'I don't want to go to Thetis Island!' She rubbed her hands uneasily down the front of her shorts. 'You tricked me into that. I——'

His face hardened. 'Jess is my child and I intend to have her in my life. And not the way you'd choose, me paying courtesy visits once in a blue moon, visiting on your turf. I'll have her in my home and I'll——'

'How do you know what I'd choose!' she shouted. She gulped and stepped back, and his hand flashed out and grasped her arm. 'Let go of me! Get your hands——'

'Step away from the damned cliff, then!'

He jerked her towards him and she tumbled against him. Her weight pressed into him, her breasts softly compressed against his chest. She gasped and pushed with both hands, gaining her balance with his heart hammering against her palms.

'I don't want——'

He backed them away from the cliff, but didn't release her. His hands were burning into her flesh. She tried to breathe shallow gulps of air, but every breath made her aware of the hardness of his body, and something in the rigid lines of his face warned her not to try to pull away.

'Would you prefer to stay behind when Jess visits me?' The way he asked the question told her that he knew the answer. He would win this battle.

'How long?' she asked. 'If we're going up there I want to know how long.'

'Let's see what happens,' he said. 'You came here to hide. There's nothing to hide from now, no need for you to live here any more.'

The ocean was red and black in the setting sun. On the cliff the house and cottage had become only shadows. 'Sue needs me,' she said. 'And Jess has friends here. And I don't——'

'Sue doesn't need you. She told me she's thinking of selling this place. And Jess will make new friends in no time.' He stared down at her, and she couldn't escape his scrutiny or his arms. He had her trapped against him, her hands pressing against his chest for freedom and her breath paced to his. 'You and Jess could move back to Thetis Island.'

'Let's by all means do things for your convenience,' she muttered. She shuddered. She could feel every breath he took, and her senses were spinning. She knew it would take nothing to push her over the edge of passion, and it would be insanity, because he would use her needs against her. 'Erase my life and replace it with your version of how it should be.' Her voice was trembling with fury. 'Why in God's name do you imagine I ran from you in the first place? Because of this—because you——'

His head blanked out the red of the sunset. Her furious breath touched his mouth and came back to her. Then his lips silenced her stammering anger with hard pressure on her mouth. She couldn't breathe. The only reality was his body against hers, his hard kiss turning gentle against her mouth. Her heart was hammering, and she knew she was lost, but she caught her hands when they curled into the tension of his chest and she pushed against him, but it felt as if she were drawing him closer as his body burned hers.

He pulled her closer and she melted against him, and the heavy seduction was dangerously strong. She ached for the heavy heat building inside her. Then he lifted his head, and it was real fear in her voice as she wailed, 'Don't touch me! Don't!'

He released her so abruptly that she staggered back from him. 'You'd better figure out what you want,' he growled. 'Your body tells a different story from your words!'

She was breathing as if she had been running. 'I don't—I don't want you. I don't love you any more!'

He cancelled her words with an angry slash of his hand on the air. 'Grow up, Dixie. It's time you realised that the world isn't some damned fairy-tale!' He stepped close and his hands stopped her when she would back away. 'Forget love, Dixie. The reality is lust, simple lust, and you can hardly deny it's there between you and me. And until you do something to change it,' he vowed softly, 'you *are* my wife. Don't forget that!'

She shook her hair back angrily, holding her body rigid against his touch. 'Have you remembered it? How many women have there been, Connar? You talk about our marriage, but you lied even as you spoke your vows. You promised love and you don't even believe in love! God knows how many times you were unfaithful to me and how——'

She tried to get away from him, but her struggle for freedom only took her closer into his embrace. Her body pressed intimately into his. As she twisted to free herself he slid his arms down her back so that her own movements forced an intimate caress of her body against his, and she froze with her breath jammed up in her throat and his mouth coming down to demand possession of her lips.

She gave it. Every breath sent her pulses thick with awareness of his body against hers. His hands at her back were bringing her into intimate contact with him, his mouth taking hers in a storm that only ended when a low whimper was torn from her throat.

When he released her she thought she might crumple to the ground. Her bones were liquid, one with her pulse. She couldn't stop staring at him, his face harsh in the last of the sun's light. She couldn't read his eyes, but his body had told her that he wanted only one thing—to take her.

She could hear his breathing. His hands were loose at his sides, but the fingers were clenched. She realised bleakly that if he had intended to prove that she still felt desire for him he'd achieved his aim. In a minute he would reach for her and she would go willingly.

When morning came she would curse herself for a fool.

'You're coming to Canada with me.' His voice was harsh.

'That was just sex,' she whispered. She clenched her hands. 'It doesn't mean anything. I won't let it mean anything.'

'I'll drag you home if I have to,' he promised. He laughed, and she shuddered, because he didn't give a damn what she wanted. 'I'm damned if I'm leaving you to run into your Alex's arms because you're afraid you'll end up in bed with me if you don't.'

She gulped and tried to stop breathing. She didn't want this primitive part of her that ached for him. 'I have commitments,' she whispered, forcing herself to sanity. 'I can't just fly away on a whim. I have to get a new run of prints done. I have a commission to do.'

He rammed his hands into his pockets. 'How long do you need?'

Forever wouldn't be long enough. 'Until the weekend,' she said.

'I'll make reservations for us to fly home on Sunday.'

'Unless a war happens in Africa or terrorists in the Middle East or——'

'Sunday,' he said grimly. 'Nothing is going to change that.'

She made a sound of derision. 'You guarantee that?'

'I guarantee it,' he said.

CHAPTER SEVEN

'WE CAN'T leave Wolf!' Jess wailed at breakfast the next morning.

'Sue will look after him,' Dixie said.

Connar overruled her. 'As long as Wolf's had his rabies shot and he's willing to fly in the baggage compartment there shouldn't be any problem bringing him.'

So while Dixie made sure that Ernie had enough prints of her pictures for her absence and hurried to finish a commission she'd undertaken to do a watercolour of an expatriate Australian's Mexican wife, Conn and Jess shopped in San Diego for a carrier for Wolf.

Sue waved goodbye to them at the airport as if Dixie and Jess were never coming back. Dixie walked aboard the plane with Connar's hand guiding her and Jess clinging to her with excitement wild in her eyes.

'This is just for a week,' Dixie reminded Connar.

Jess sat at the window seat with Connar beside her. Dixie was in the aisle seat on Conn's other side. He had seated them that way automatically as if he remembered her saying years ago, 'It was exciting visiting Daddy in Paris, but every time I looked out of the window I thought what would happen if the plane fell. Next time I'm sitting in the aisle seat.'

She hadn't been on a plane since then. She'd taken the bus from Vancouver to Seattle when she ran from

Connar, then the train to San Diego. There hadn't been any need to fly.

It wasn't reasonable that Connar had remembered her nervousness. But he had, and she sat stiffly beside him when her seatbelt was done up, knowing she was going to lose this battle. The moment would come when he reached for her with serious intent and she would be in his bed and his life and whatever happened would happen. She'd lose control of herself and she would spend eternity waiting for him to return to her. Then one day on television she would watch the end and she would never be whole again.

'A week,' she said again. 'When we get to Vancouver I'm making reservations for the return flight.' Connar had booked return tickets but left the return reservations open.

He didn't reply, and she spent much of the three-hour flight promising herself she wouldn't stay one hour longer than a week. No matter what Connar did.

'Give me your papers,' Connar demanded as the plane landed. He held his hand out for her Canadian birth certificate and Jess's Mexican one.

Connar took charge of the red tape at Immigration in a businesslike fashion. Along with the papers that testified to Jess's entitlement to Canadian citizenship Conn produced the seven-year-old document that marked his marriage to Dixie Bradshaw.

'My wife and daughter,' he announced, indicating they'd been living outside the country. He shrugged off the immigration man's disapproval at their not registering Jess's birth with the Canadian authorities. 'We'll look after it now that they're home,' he said, and Dixie felt the same weariness that had haunted her ever since Connar proposed this visit.

Of course she would look after registering Jess's birth in Canada now—although she suspected Conn would have that formality looked after before she had a chance to figure out how it was done. What bothered her was the fact that Connar talked as if they were home to stay, the way he said, 'My wife and daughter,' as if they'd been a family always.

Jess kept watching him with worshipful eyes. 'What about Wolf?' she asked, and Conn reassured her that they would see Wolf shortly.

'What about the taxi?' asked Dixie. 'Wolf and the taxi?' It would take a tolerant taxi driver to accept a large, wild-looking dog as a passenger.

'No problem,' said Conn, and a few moments later he ushered them into a long white limousine.

Jess talked non-stop. When they settled into the limousine with Wolf lying on the floor between the seats she demanded to know, 'What kind of car is this?' When they went through the George Massey Tunnel under the Fraser River she demanded, 'What's this big cave?' Connar explained patiently.

When they got out of the limo Wolf was returned to his cage for the ferry trip to Vancouver Island. The ferry was a new high-speed catamaran that left from downtown Vancouver, not the slower car-ferry Dixie was accustomed to. Jess asked the names of everything, from the islands they passed to the parts of the ferry. Conn answered with a lazy air of amusement. His ease with his daughter was only another strand in the net that was closing in around Dixie.

A visit, he'd said, but to the immigration officer he'd said, 'My wife,' as if it were a permanent thing. One night seven years ago hardly made a marriage, but she hadn't denied the relationship when Conn was talking to the immigration official. And although she'd vowed she would make their return reservation the instant they landed on Canadian soil, Conn had guided her through the airport terminal and she'd been nowhere near the airline ticket counters.

She told herself it was only habit for her to do things Conn's way, but it was a habit she'd better break, or she would end up trapped in marriage with a man who wanted her primarily because she was the mother of his child. She understood well enough that he intended to be a real father to Jess, but how could she make a life with him when the only reason was convenience and physical compatibility?

When she got to his house, to a telephone, she would call for reservations. She would feel safer with a definite date for their return, an anchor against whatever *he* planned for their future.

When they arrived on Vancouver Island Wolf was again freed from his cage. Connar let him into the back seat of a dark Mercedes that couldn't be more than a year old. 'You don't mind sharing the back seat with Wolf?' he asked Jess.

'Nope! I don't mind.' Jess clambered after the dog, her eyes wide and filled with a day that had taken her from Mexico to Canada.

'She's going to need a nap,' said Dixie.

He slung a suitcase into the boot of the car. 'She might drop off in the car.'

'You're into status cars,' Dixie said, touching the shiny surface of the Mercedes.

'Comfort,' he corrected, smiling slightly. 'You look as if you could use a nap too. Let's go catch that last ferry over to Thetis Island.'

It disconcerted her that he'd seen her exhaustion when she was working so hard not to show anything on her face. He got into the car and tossed her a glance that stripped away the mask she tried to wear. 'Why don't you try for a bit of sleep? Use my shoulder if you like.'

She edged away from him, and he laughed softly. She sat stiffly all the way to the ferry that serviced Thetis Island and then all the way across the little harbour that took her back home.

'Do you want to get out?' he asked on the ferry. 'Stand on deck?'

'No.' She turned away from him, remembering a teenage Connar standing at her side as she'd stood at the front of the ferry in the toughest weather. She had lifted her hands to feel the salt spray as the ferry hit the waves, had shouted, 'You'll catch me if a wave takes me, won't you, Conn?'

She might have been ten years old then. At ten she'd believed in fantasies that said she'd grow up to be the princess of Thetis Island and Connar would marry her one day because he loved her more than anyone else in the world.

She yawned and he said, 'My shoulder's still here.'

'No, thanks.' She wasn't going to sleep until she had a door to close against Connar. She could visualise herself waking from daytime sleep with her traitorous body melted against his. And if he looked down at her and kissed her and touched her face with one long gentle finger...

He would take her readily enough if she offered. He'd done it before. He'd loved her body and left her heart empty. 'I love you,' she'd declared intensely on their wedding night. He'd left her love unanswered, and it had taken her years to train herself not to love Connar Stanford.

If she let herself need him now she might lose every inch she had gained. She might come to pieces in his arms. Then morning would come and he would walk away without looking back. He said she was his wife, but he wasn't offering her any of the things she needed.

Like love. Like a real partnership. And if she was tempted to dream that it might be different this time, she had only to look at Connar's behaviour. He'd demanded that they come to Thetis Island without caring what it might do to her life. And while she said she would stay a week he was introducing her to everyone as his wife.

If she walked into Connar's arms a second time...

She had to be insane if she let that happen. He was the man who said love was just a word. It wasn't love she felt for Connar Stanford. A long time ago she'd had a severe childhood case of hero-worship. She'd let it turn into love then, but she knew better now.

As Connar drove off the ferry the only sounds in the car were Wolf whimpering in his sleep and Jess snoring softly as if her nose was stuffy—and the car's muted engine. Connar eased gently along the winding road and finally into his own lane.

'You've had it resurfaced,' she said.

'Last year,' he said. He turned off the lane just before the farmhouse.

'Where are you going?'

'I gave the old house to Wayne—the new man I hired to look after the farm.' He was driving along a new section of road where there had been only long grass when she was a child. 'I'd always wanted to build my own place.'

'By the harbour,' she breathed, remembering how he'd sat astride a big log on the beach and used his hands to describe for her the house he would one day build for himself.

She thought it was bigger than what he'd planned when he'd been seventeen, telling her about the summer hideaway he would build on Thetis Island. 'I won't live there all the time,' he'd explained then. 'I'll be off on the other side of the world most of the time, so it would be silly to make the place too big.'

He'd made it more than comfortable. A two-storey house with a long living-room facing out over the water, a veranda running all around the house and chairs at a small table at the back. She could imagine him sitting out there with his eyes on the trees and herself in the chair across from him.

She scrambled out of the car stiffly when it stopped.

'Go ahead in,' he suggested. 'I'll get Jess and the bags.'

'It'll be locked.'

'Not here,' he said, and more than anything that made her realise how far she'd gone from this place where she'd once dreamed of living her whole life. 'Not here'. No need to lock doors in this tiny island community where she'd grown up.

Wolf ran past and she swung to watch him, one hand stretched out as if to pull him back. 'Shouldn't we tie him?'

'He'll be fine,' Conn said patiently. 'Go ahead.'

'I'll wait for you.'

He was bending down to lift Jess out of the back seat. Her daughter mumbled and squirmed and then sagged back into sleep as Conn stood erect with her in his arms. Dixie felt pain clench in her chest at the sight of them together.

She followed Conn slowly up the three stairs to the veranda. She reached past him and turned the knob, and as the door swung open silently she jerked her hand back from the accidental contact with Conn's hip.

She wasn't positive it was accidental. Maybe her subconscious...

She stepped inside and was surrounded by warm natural cedars on the walls, hardwood floors and soft carpeting. Connar walked straight upstairs with a sleeping Jess in his arms and Wolf at his heels.

'Wolf——'

'He's OK. Relax, Dixie.'

The last thing she could let herself do was to relax. She prowled the house, with the slight sounds of Connar's footsteps coming from upstairs. The living-room was all warm earth tones from the walls to the lush carpet that covered the hardwood floor. The big kitchen had evening light pouring through glass patio doors. The breakfast nook was cosy with a glass table and wicker chairs and a notice-board where Conn had tacked up an assortment of notes.

'Harry: 27th, Berlin.'

'Call Jacobs about Taiwan.'

'Tom—June 1.'

This island hideaway didn't represent the real Connar. The real man was there on the bulletin board. Berlin…Taiwan…and New York, because Conn had mentioned something about his network chief, and the man's name was Tom. She might look at this house and see a home, but when Conn looked at it he probably saw that bulletin board. She knew him. He would never stay in one place or give his heart to anything that trapped him. That was why he hadn't loved her. Because love was a trap.

She left the notice-board with its reminders of reality and walked through the back section of the house. She found a room that was probably intended as a family room, but was obviously not much used. Then a closed door. When she opened it she stepped out of elegant country living into the modern world: computer terminal, fax machine, video machine and television screen, books from floor to ceiling, and she browsed the titles until she came to the section where he'd shelved an endless selection of video tapes. They weren't movies, of course. News broadcasts. Documentaries. She read the labels on the spine. You could close the door on this room and forget there were trees and an ocean just outside.

This room and the bulletin board were the real Connar. The rest of the house was atmosphere. She might dream that she could reach him out there in the living-room, but if he was inside this room she wouldn't have a chance

Or out there when a telephone rang. Despite the fire in his eyes and the way his heart had hammered when he held her close, all it would take was one ring of the telephone to tear Connar away from her. And it was a good thing that she'd never got round to applying for identification in Connar's name when she married him, because keeping her maiden name was going to save her a major hassle when the divorce came.

Dixie Stanford. Years ago when he said they should get married she'd been fool enough to write that version of her name again and again on a piece of paper. As if writing his name blended with hers would guarantee love. Even then she must have known subconsciously that the dream of a marriage with Connar was a faulted fantasy.

He wanted his daughter, but he wasn't cruel enough to try to tear Jess away from her mother. He thought he knew a better way. He planned to stay married to her. Some time during this *visit* he would ask her to stay, to allow him to have the family he said he wanted.

If she agreed, then they would share a daughter and a bed. But there would be nothing he felt for her that he hadn't felt for other women. Just lust. He'd made that plain enough. Nothing special. Nothing unique.

'How many women?' she'd asked him back in Ensenada. He hadn't answered.

She heard him coming down the stairs, heard him walking through the rooms until he found her. She turned slowly, and for a second she saw that his face was lined with weariness. Then it was gone. Would she ever understand him?

No. Not unless he wanted her to.

She spread her fingers across the fabric of her trousers on her upper thighs, then clenched them when she saw his gaze drop to the nervous gesture of her hands. 'Is Jess sleeping?' she asked.

'Yes. Go up and get some sleep yourself.' He touched her shoulder so fleetingly that she had no chance to jerk away. 'Yours is the first room on the right upstairs.'

She was crazy to think of anything but a divorce. That was the only way she could deal with Connar Stanford. Separated. Divorced, finally and forever. She walked across to his big mahogany desk. On a shelf beside the desk were telephone books for a variety of places: Vancouver; Toronto; New York; a small one for the area including Thetis Island. She pulled out the Vancouver book, and it took her only a moment to find the number she needed.

There was a telephone on his desk. She dialled and stood with her eyes locked on Connar's as the ringing tone sounded in her ear. She made reservations for herself and Jess while Conn stood five feet away listening. Then she hung up the telephone.

'Reservations can be cancelled,' he said.

That night in the darkness she woke with those words in her ears. 'Reservations can be cancelled'. She shivered, although there was warm spring air coming through the open window. Connar's eyes, Connar's voice telling her more than the words said. That he would turn things his own way... cancel her plans for her life... cancel her future and mould it to his desires.

When she woke the next morning she found Jess's room empty and the bed untidily made. There were two other doors leading off the upstairs corridor. She wasn't certain which was Connar's, and she certainly wasn't about to go prowling. The last thing she wanted was to open a door and find herself staring at Connar Stanford's bed!

She heard voices and followed the sound downstairs. She found Connar in the kitchen, cooking bacon and eggs at the modern electric stove. Jess was at the counter, dropping toast in the toaster.

'I'm buttering it too,' her daughter announced with pride, gesturing towards a small stack of toast irregularly slathered in butter. Dixie saw Connar smother a grin.

'Connar likes toast,' Dixie said. 'Especially if it's drowning in butter.'

He laughed. Someone knocked on the door and he shouted, 'Come!'

The kitchen was invaded by a middle-aged woman Dixie had never seen before.

'Yvonne Stannish,' said Connar. 'She and her husband Wayne have leased the farmland from me the last few years. Yvonne, I'd like you to meet my wife Dixie. And Jess, my daughter.'

What could Dixie say? I'm not his wife? I'm leaving next week? Yvonne swept over and gave her an enthusiastic hug, then started telling Jess how her own grandchildren were visiting for the summer and dying for someone their age to play with.

'Would you like me to look after your meals?' she asked Dixie. 'Good idea, eh?'

'Yes, please,' said Conn. 'I've promised Dixie a vacation.' He smiled as if at a private joke between man and wife. 'And my wife is a better artist than a cook.'

Dixie wished she could have thrown something at him, but Yvonne and Jess were both watching her. Yvonne must have wondered just what kind of marriage this could be. She must have heard rumours. Everyone on Thetis Island knew that Connar had brought Dixie home as his wife seven years ago. They must also know that she'd disappeared the next day.

'I'll be down later, then,' Yvonne said. 'When the little one has had breakfast why don't you send her up to the farm to meet my lot—or shall I send them down?'

In the end they came down, seven-year-old twins named Gary and Wendy. They carried Jess off to the play area up behind the farmhouse where they said there was a swing and a super playhouse.

'They'll be fine,' said Conn, as if he felt Dixie's tension.

'All right,' agreed Dixie, and the twins led Jess off. By the time they were out of sight up the hill Jess was echoing their whooping shouts. Wolf ran beside Jess, barking excitedly.

Dixie started picking up the plates from the table.

'Yvonne will get those later,' he said.

She ignored him and stacked the knives and forks on top of the plates. 'What about this toast?' she asked.

'We'll compost it.'

She smiled unwillingly. 'Twenty years ago we'd be upset about the waste. But now a compost pile makes a virtue of waste.' He didn't answer, and she put the plate down sharply. She could feel him watching her. 'Conn...?'

Silence. He was very still, as if he were waiting for something.

'You're letting everyone think we're married.' She couldn't tell what he was thinking, but his eyes flared, her clue that there was more on his mind than she could see in his face.

'We are married,' he said. 'Or have you forgotten the promises you made to me in that church seven years ago?'

'You made promises too. You said words you couldn't possibly have meant. You...' She gulped and whispered, 'Damn you, Conn! It was my damned life you took when you married me!'

'You talk as if I dragged you into that church.' He lifted his head, and she felt danger on the air.

She flushed with the memory of her old dreams. 'We're not man and wife. Not now. Seven years and we... The way you're talking, everyone thinks... The customs man and Yvonne and—and Jess! You're teaching Jess to have expectations, and I don't want her hurt.'

He stepped towards her and she backed away. His hand touched her arm and she wanted to shake it off, but somehow even that expression of will was impossible with his gaze probing her face. 'What expectations?' he demanded. 'That her father is going to be part of her life? I intend to be. No child of mine is going to grow up not knowing her father.'

'Your father...' What did she know about his father? Only that Aunt Jessie never mentioned his name. No pictures. No mention of him.

'We're talking about Jess.'

She didn't know how it could be, but in all those years living with Aunt Jessie and Connar she'd never heard Connar's father mentioned once. She parted her lips to protest his changing the subject, but he wasn't going to answer her questions. That was part of the reality.

'Conn, we can't possibly pretend that this is a normal family. I know we have to make some arrangement about you seeing Jess and——'

His hand tightened on her shoulder. 'You're going to stay,' he said. 'That's the only reasonable arrangement.'

She shook her head and gulped panic.

His jaw seemed to harden. 'This man back in Mexico. Alex. *Is* he your lover?'

'No,' she whispered, because it seemed ludicrous to pretend she yearned for another man when she knew that if Conn only kissed her or brought her close to him...or simply kept staring into her eyes like that... If he did any of those things she would melt.

'You've always liked it here. It hasn't changed.' He gestured towards the water that was visible through the patio doors.

'I've changed.' His touch was on her and she couldn't seem to pull free of it. 'I've learned to be free. I won't be put back into a cage.'

He dropped his hand. 'Is that how you see it?'

She stepped back. She felt frightened and had no clear idea of exactly what it was she feared. He was so silent, watching her, probably evaluating her words and her expression in that computer behind his eyes and coming up with an answer as to how he could manipulate her to get what he wanted.

He wouldn't give up.

'How long until the phone rings?' she asked desperately. She told herself to turn and get out of this room, get outside, because there was something in the air that might make her say crazy things. 'You've been away from it all for days now, more than a week. So how long, Connar?'

'Away from what?' His voice was so soft that it felt threatening.

'Away from all of it—your world.' She had the feeling that she was one of his interview subjects, that he was leading her towards a trap. She flung her hands out. 'What will it be, Conn? Trouble in Africa again? If I'd stayed around, how long would it have taken for you to remember you had a wife?'

She laughed, and his face got grimmer and he didn't answer, just waited for her to say more.

'Shall we make a bet on what it will take this time? It won't take much, will it? The echo of a gun fired in Africa. Rumour of a riot in Europe. You talk as if this were your home, but it's not. You want to trap us here so we're around when you remember to care. But you'll go with the first ring of that telephone. And we'll be here like fish in a tank or...'

She gulped back a flood of screaming words. His face might have been carved in stone. 'Don't you ever shout back?' she demanded shakily.

'There won't be any phone calls,' he said in a flat voice. 'I'm on a leave of absence while I write a book.'

'A book?' She thought of the office and all those tapes, the computer and the fax machine. 'What kind of book? You're writing it here?'

'About television news. And yes, I'm writing it here.'

'Is it going well?' She felt as if she'd just made a fool of herself and wasn't sure exactly why, except that she'd been screaming and Connar had been as calm as the big rock out at the point.

'Well enough. Some people won't like the result when it's published.'

She could believe that. Connar always seemed to see through the images to the real truth. It was a talent that had made him famous, and it might be why he had survived experiences that would have killed most men.

'I'm sorry I screamed at you. I just . . . I sometimes feel as if you don't hear me.'

His eyes narrowed. 'I may not like what you say, but I hear you, Dixie. And at least when you're screaming I know I'm getting your real thoughts, not the mask you wear.'

She grimaced. 'I can't do this, Connar. A whole week. I—I might murder you.'

He smiled. 'I'll try not to make that necessary. Why don't we try to pretend that we don't have to be on guard with each other? Give it a week, then if you must you can take up arms against me again.'

'But——'

'I'll be in my office.' He turned away abruptly. 'Do whatever you want. I'll see you at lunch.'

The sound of his office door closing rang through the house.

Damn Connar! If she followed him he would be buried in the details of the book he was writing. Pretend they didn't need to be on guard? Impossible!

A week without fighting and she'd be lost. It was the antagonism that kept her safe. Without it he would win in a minute, and she dared not let him persuade her to stay. He *would* leave when the book was done.

She could bear that if he loved her, if he would ache to be back with her when he was on the other side of the world...yearn for the time apart to be gone.

She had to survive this week and get away from him. It wouldn't be easy. He knew the power he had over her. Sexual power. He felt it too, but he seemed to have no problem controlling his desire when he wished to. Lust. The same emotion he had felt for Elsie all those years ago in the long grass down in the hollow near the water. She didn't mean any more to him than Elsie had...or Sonya.

But one day there might be a woman he loved. Her vision blurred with suppressed tears as she forced herself to face that fact. Whether he admitted it or not, Connar was a man of fierce passions—the passion to know the truth, the passion to reveal it! His book would be filled with restrained passion, and one day he could love a woman with that same intensity. And if there was a hell on this world, Dixie would know it intimately if she had to watch Connar fall in love with some other woman.

CHAPTER EIGHT

WITH Connar buried in the office, Dixie walked up the hill to check on Jess. She found all three children huddled in the playhouse with an oddball assortment of dolls and Tonka trucks. Wolf was lying at the entrance.

'He's guarding for us,' explained Jess.

'Case o' burglars,' added Gary.

'Good idea,' said Dixie.

'These guys have hundreds of trucks,' Jess announced.

'I can see that,' said Dixie. 'Have fun.'

Jess was obviously having a great time and didn't need her mother hovering. Dixie went back down the hillside, avoiding the path that would make her visible from the farmhouse windows. She didn't want to be invited in for coffee and a chat. Yvonne might not have asked Connar any questions—most people weren't too quick to question Connar. But the woman probably wouldn't hesitate to question Dixie if she got her alone.

She went down to the water. It must be one of the highest tides of the spring. Even the logs up against the trees were floating. She watched one log for a long time, trying to catch the moment when the tide turned. As always, the change was too slow for her to detect it. She'd lost bets with Connar in the past over this, telling him the tide was going down while he proved a moment later that the water was still rising. She was too often fooled by the movement of the waves, while Connar seemed to see past the little waves to the larger reality.

The story of her life, she thought wryly, making mistakes because she couldn't see the real truth. Like marrying Connar. Except that if she hadn't she would never have had Jess, and she couldn't imagine her life without Jess.

She went back to Conn's house for her sketchpad. When she returned to the beach the tide had dropped just enough that some of the logs were anchored in sand again. She began to sketch, and somehow time got away from her until Connar's voice called her to lunch. She'd lost herself in the reflections of the sun on the glassy water... the way the long grass grew in the water at high tide... the masts of a sailboat streaking in a distorted reflection as the water rippled.

Yvonne had brought down a platter of sandwiches and a tureen of home-made split pea soup for their lunch. Jess had come with her. 'Shepherd's pie for supper,' Yvonne announced. 'That is, if you all like shepherd's pie.'

'Is it like apple pie?' asked Jess.

Connar laughed, and Dixie felt herself smiling with him as she explained to Jess that shepherd's pie had meat and potatoes instead of apples and pastry.

'But you *will* like it,' she assured her, and somehow Connar's smile warmed Dixie instead of making her feel endangered. He went back into his office after lunch, and when Jess ran off to rejoin the twins Dixie went back to her sketching.

The days slipped past slowly. Connar often worked on his book in the office, but sometimes he lazed on a lawn chair while he edited pages of manuscript. On the second day Dixie sketched him frowning over words on paper while Wolf lay at his feet and the late afternoon sun made everything brilliantly contrasted. She stared at the sketch and hoped it wouldn't hurt to look at it when this was over.

Five days left. Five days until their flight home.

The next afternoon when the sun began to drop lower in the sky Conn suggested a swim to douse the heat. The three of them went into the cool water in the bay. Conn took Jess up on his shoulders, and she shrieked encouragement as he walked out until the water was up to his shoulders. With Jess straddling his shoulders and hanging on with hands laced into his hair, Conn called back to Dixie, who had just taken a photograph of them.

'What about you, Dix? Want a ride?'

'No way!' she shouted, moving back to put the camera down.

She dived into the water and swam hard out to the raft, but she could not escape the images in her mind. He'd taken her for rides like that when she was young, his hands holding her legs as she sat on his shoulders, the water climbing up as he walked. But it would be different if he carried her through the water now.

She would be aware in a way she'd never been then. She would feel every flex of the muscles in his shoulders. Then ... when they were deep and he sank down into the water she would float free until he caught her. He would pull her close and they would drop down together with the water closing over them as his mouth drank deeply from hers. Then . . .

Damn! She had to stop this!

She stood up on the raft and quickly dived in over the side. Then she swam until she was exhausted, but when she went to bed that night she dreamed the fantasy she'd tried to suppress: Connar loving her in the water.

Four days left. Four endless days.

'Can I read it?' she asked him the next day.

He was sitting in the lawn chair with manuscript all around. He looked up and stared at her as if she had come from another planet.

'Forget it,' she said, standing up so quickly that she felt dizzy. She'd been lounging in a chaise, watching him while her mind wandered. The sun . . . another hot, lazy day . . . the sound of Jess's laughter from up the hill . . . a cow bawling out in the fields . . . Conn frowning as he made a mark on a page of manuscript.

He glanced down at the papers he held. 'How do you feel when someone asks to see your unfinished work?' he asked idly.

'Defensive,' she admitted.

'There you are,' he said lightly. 'I can't risk it.'

That was nonsense, and they both knew it. 'What you can't risk is intimacy,' she muttered.

His eyes narrowed. 'How do you get that?'

'You're good at asking questions, but you're rotten at answering them.' She bit her lip, because it was too easy for this kind of conversation to backfire on her with Connar. 'It seems to me that you'd risk your life before you'd risk letting me know what you're thinking.'

'If you want answers you'll have to have the guts to ask the questions out loud.' He lifted the sheaf of papers. 'This isn't a biography. The only answers in here are about television news.'

Three days left.

'Come for a walk?' he asked the next evening.

They had just put Jess to bed. There had been a salmon barbecue at the community centre and Jess had fallen asleep in the back of the car on the way home, but had insisted when she woke that she wanted Connar to read her a bedtime story, even though it was way past her usual bedtime.

Conn had read a story from a book Dixie remembered from her own childhood, and Jess had fallen asleep some time in the middle of the third page. Dixie had stood at the window, looking out on the reflections of moonlight on water and listening to his voice. When he stopped reading she turned and watched him place the closed book on the bedside table.

'She fell asleep pages ago,' said Dixie.

'I know. I like watching her.' He was smiling. 'Besides, last night when I stopped reading she opened her eyes and said I was cheating. I was supposed to read the whole story.' His voice was low and amused, but his eyes were shadowed as he said, 'Come for a walk? We need to talk.'

About what? About Jess? Or about the disaster that had started with an exchange of vows in a church in Vancouver? She didn't ask, which proved Connar was right. She didn't have the guts to ask the questions, even though she needed the answers.

She followed him out of the room and down the stairs. The world outside was black and white with

'Sudden, isn't it, this passion for Alex?' The grimness in his voice acted as cold water on her flesh.

She shuddered and stepped down towards the water. The air felt cold. It was only the beginning of summer, and without the sun to warm her it would be a shock to dive into the black mirror of water in front of her.

'What are you doing?' he demanded.

'Going swimming,' she said.

'It's too cold. Dixie...'

She scrambled over the log and found the beach white in the light from the sky. He said something and she thought he was coming after her. His hand would stretch out and pull her back. It was the water or the man, and something like a laugh came from her throat, only it wasn't a laugh and she didn't know what it was, but it turned to a gasp as she kicked off her sandals and the water hit her ankles. She ran three strides into it and the cold curled around her thighs.

'It's lovely!' she called back.

Then she dived forward, and the heat on her flesh shattered as the ocean flowed over her. She turned and stood and it was waist-high, cold water all around her and the sea sheeting off her body as she walked slowly through clinging water towards Connar.

He was standing at the water's edge, a stern figure with moonlight on his face and impatience in every line of his body. She shivered deeply and took another step towards him. A soft breath of wind curled around the clinging wetness of her tank top.

'Come out,' he said. 'You're freezing.'

She laughed again, and it was madness in her veins. 'Afraid to come in after me?' she taunted, but he didn't react. She walked another step through the water, as if his gaze had pulled her towards him. 'I suppose you think I'm behaving very childishly,' she said. The ocean was all around her and she could feel the storm inside too. She might scream at him or run against him to pummel his chest with angry fists. Anger was boiling, and she wasn't sure why.

'There's wildness in you tonight,' he said, 'but there's nothing childlike about it.'

She came another step, and she was standing ankle-deep in water, and he was two steps away. 'If I leave on Sunday will you try to take Jess away from me?'

'You're not leaving.' He reached and she thought it was too far, but his hand took her arm and she realised then that he had come into the water. She stared down at the water around them, and his touch was on her, but she felt nothing.

'Your shoes will get wet,' she said numbly.

He pulled her close and she was shivering against the hardness of his chest, his hands rubbing her arms, and she felt the numbness turning into burning. He bent to pick her up, and she jerked back in his grasp.

'Don't! Don't——'

'Damn you,' he muttered. 'Do you have any idea what you want?'

'Yes.' The shivering was going deeper inside her, making her voice tremble. 'I want to be free of you. I want to have my own life. I want...' He swung her into his arms and she gulped, but the shivering was consuming her and she whispered shakily, 'The wind's come up.'

'Yes, you fool! And you're freezing.' She heard the water splashing around his feet, and then the trees were all around and he was climbing the hill. She thought she could feel his heart beating, but the shaking of her body rivalled it.

'I want to be—b—be free of you.' She managed to hold her head up. If it touched his shoulder she knew it would be a defeat, that she would have no fight left. 'I want—to watch tele—television without seeing—without caring if you—I want...'

He carried her up the stairs to the veranda and she saw the swing seat and lost herself in a fantasy of lying there with the swing moving gently and Connar's hands on her face. She whimpered and closed her eyes tightly.

His body was tight and hard with the tension moonlight showed on his face. She felt him shift her weight and then the sound of a door opening. 'For God's sake,' he muttered. 'Can't we do this without tearing each other apart?'

She opened her eyes and there was light.

He pushed the door of the downstairs bathroom open and lowered her to her feet. Her teeth were chattering and she clamped them together to stop the sound. He was angry. His jaw was rigid and his eyes grim. His hands were abruptly efficient, and she stood helpless and shivering while he stripped the clothes from her like a child. She tried to cover herself, her arms wrapping around her breasts to hide nipples puckered from the cold. He brushed her hands away and she whimpered.

'Do you imagine I'm going to hurt you?' She saw a spasm in his throat as he turned away from her. He pulled a big towel from a shelf and wrapped her in it so that her arms were pinned at her sides. She wasn't warm, but when she let her jaw relax the chattering had stopped.

'Conn...?'

He took another towel and began methodically to dry her hair. She was glad when he turned her away from him, because she could stop staring at the impatience in his face. He sat on the edge of the bath and drew her back against him so that she was standing with her back to him, cradled between his legs. The towel around her slipped, and she tangled her fingers in it from inside to stop it falling.

'I'm sorry,' she said numbly. 'That was a stupid thing to do.'

He didn't answer. She supposed silence was answer enough.

She drew her bottom lip between her teeth and then released it. 'I'm OK now. You can stop,' she said, but she didn't want him to stop. The gentle rhythm of his hands through the towel was soothing. She closed her eyes and her senses reached for the ending of it. She heard the sound of the small towel dropping to the floor. Then his fingers were in her hair as if he were combing it with his hands.

'What am I going to do with you?' he asked in an oddly ragged voice.

'I don't know,' she whispered. She could feel the tension in his thighs. She thought of how he had stripped her, his face hard as he made her naked. How could he take her clothes and feel nothing? 'I got you wet, didn't I?'

'It doesn't matter,' he said.

She moved experimentally, and there was nothing holding her. She couldn't turn to face him. She stared at her own image in the mirror and would not let her eyes see the man behind her. 'I think it's time I went to bed.'

He held the door open for her. She managed to get into the corridor without looking up at him, but she had to pass so close to him that she could breathe in his scent, and she trembled and stopped with her back to him and his shadow lying over hers ahead of her. He said her name.

When his words came they were so quiet that she wasn't sure they were real. She stopped and lifted her head and she knew that she was lost, that there had never been a choice from the moment she saw him across the crowd in the mall back in San Diego.

'What did you say?' Her voice should have been trembling, but it wasn't. It was steady, but so husky that it must sound deliberately seductive. She turned around, and he was watching her in a way that made her aware of the fact that although the towel over her shoulders was massive enough to drown her shape it would take only one touch from him to strip it away.

'I said—if you're going to bed . . . then make it my bed.'

She stared at him and tried to read past his mask. 'Why?' she asked. Do you love me? She *couldn't* ask that. If a woman had to ask, the answer would never be the one she needed. She moved away from him and walked towards the open front door.

He followed her.

'I want to sit on the swing,' she said breathlessly.

'This has to stop,' he said. He touched her and turned her to face him. She could see the dampness from her wet body everywhere on him. He was almost as wet as she had been. Angry, she had thought from his voice, but it wasn't anger in his eyes as they searched her face and settled on the trembling that was her mouth.

'Are you going to kiss me?' Her voice was hardly any sound at all.

'If I do——' his head lifted and he watched her through narrowed eyes '—it won't end there, Dixie.'

She touched his chest with one hand. The towel slipped and she reached to save it, but his arms surrounded her and pinned the towel to her body, pinned her body against his.

His lips were cool. She breathed in the scent of ocean mingled with the faintest echo of the aftershave he used. She wanted to watch him as he kissed her, to keep her eyes open and read his face. But his lips moved from her mouth to her eyes and he pressed the lids closed with feather touches from his lips, so that her breath went out on a long sigh.

'I'm taking you upstairs.' His words were a soft breath against her skin.

'No,' she pleaded.

She thought of the long stairs and of Connar carrying her as if he owned her, taking her as he must have known he would when he brought her here. She backed away from him, backed up until she was against the open door that led outside. She saw a shadow from a moth that had fluttered into the house. It was fluttering around a lamp in the living-room. She turned and stepped out on to the veranda and wondered where she thought she was going.

She sat on the swing. She heard the sound of the door closing, Connar closing the door. Then silence.

She stared out at the shadows that led to the water and felt intense awareness that he was still standing at the door, one hand on the knob, as if he might go back in and leave her out here alone.

'The moon's gone behind a cloud,' she whispered.

'Why are you running from me?' His quiet voice blended with the night.

'Because I'm afraid.' It was dark out here. Time for truth in the dark.

'Of me?' His shadow moved between her and the water. 'Or afraid of yourself because you want me as much as I want you?'

She looked up at him and knew the answer. She had claimed that she had run away because of the life he led, because he didn't love her. But the deepest fear had been that he would make her need him with a depth that would leave her helpless to survive when he left her.

Could she give her body to him now and keep her heart intact? Somehow she must, because he was only a breath away, and she knew this was one time she wasn't capable of running away.

'Make love to me,' she whispered.

He was motionless, staring at her in shadows.

'Do you think I'll run again?' Her voice had gone husky. She let her hands loose, and the towel slid free of her shoulders. 'I'm not running,' she breathed.

He sat down beside her. He didn't touch her. 'Do you know what you're doing this time?'

She touched the dampness of his shirt. 'You're wet. You'll catch cold.' Her fingers tangled in the place where the first button was fastened. She loosened it and then another. His flesh underneath felt hot and dry. She pressed her hand against it and felt the roughness of curling hair, the hammering of his heart. 'You want me,' she said, staring at her own hand. She remembered Elsie in his arms years ago and pushed the vision away. 'I know you do.' She drew her lower lip between her teeth as her fingers unfastened another button.

He reached for her. A shudder tore through her as his fingers touched the curve of her breast. 'Connar...'

'Witch,' he growled. 'I promised myself I wouldn't do this unless——'

She tilted her head back and let her body lean against his touch. 'Don't talk,' she begged. She felt his palm brush against her breast, and her breath caught. His own breathing tore as if he felt her response deep inside himself. She moved and felt him against her and felt something snap in him, and she melted into his hardness. Passion, she told herself desperately. Only sex. Her heart was still her own.

His hands were roughly gentle. They slid along the nakedness of her shoulders to draw her into him so that she lost her breath against him and her breasts crushed into the hardness of his chest. His mouth settled on to hers and she gave herself to him, opening as his lips probed hers. She led his tongue on as it invaded. Her dark pulse drew him in with need, flowing ahead of his possession so that she could not separate her heartbeat from his.

His hands moved down her back, moulding her body to his. He moved away from her, and she whimpered in protest. 'No,' she breathed, but then his hand took her breast and the sound in her throat told him her needs as his mouth moved along the softness. The dizziness swallowed her, and she grasped desperately for the last sanity. His touch was on her naked body, and the madness was tearing free from where she had kept it locked all these years.

'It's all right,' he promised.

Yes, because she would give him only her body. Only passion. Not love. He kissed the softness of her breast, and she twisted and took his body over hers, heavy on hers, so that each breath she took crushed her under his weight and a primitive force deep inside her pushed wildly against his weight, his male power, taunting it and needing it and begging him to take her beyond her heartbeat.

His tongue was on her nipple. She cried out and he lifted her with his hands so that she was bent back in his arms, her back arched and his mouth on her breasts and a cry tearing at her throat. He made a sound like a growl and took her sounds into his mouth, and then his weight left her and he was kneeling beside the swing sofa and stroking the last remnant of the towel from her with long, slow caresses that burned down the fiery pulsing of her body from her breasts to her thighs and back, and slowing as her breath tore through her, and his mouth was on her and his voice deep and unsteady.

She touched him with wildness. Her trembling hands fought the barrier of fabric over his skin, and then it was gone and he came down over her with flesh against her thighs and her breasts and her mouth hungry against his shoulder.

'It's too late,' he groaned against her mouth, his tongue taking hers and his body burning hers. His hand stroked her hip and she arched against him and told him with a sound that had no form what it was she ached for.

'You can't leave me now,' he growled.

His words were sounds without sense. She buried her hands in his hair and gave everything into the kiss, and she drew him against her thighs and tangled her legs in his and felt his hard need pulsing in the instant before possession. Then he moved and she cried out and the madness was real and alive and the flames took the last breath of covering from her heart.

CHAPTER NINE

IT WAS a dream, the kind of dream that seduced with its reality. His body over hers and the wildness beyond anything that could exist in the real world, as if her very breath cried to his and her pulse beat inside him, his in her.

His sounds against her flesh . . . her answers. The pulses wild and the flames everywhere . . . the scent of her own cries in her nostrils . . . the sound of sea salt in her ears . . . the sensation of eternity beating in her veins.

Connar deep inside her . . . driving the flames into a long explosion that took her apart into pieces that could never come together again . . . sensation beyond feeling and the thunder of heart and skin and breath gone too far . . . draining away into the pulse of a long, slow slide back down the night in his arms.

His body heavy on hers. She tasted the flesh of his shoulder, and it was the flavour of her dream. He shifted and she was lying against him, still possessed by him in the echo of passion. She breathed, and perhaps it was his name she whispered, but the sound had no form.

'Don't talk,' he said huskily. He threaded his fingers into her hair and pressed her face against his chest. She felt his heartbeat and heard his breath slowing as his pulse moved back from the pace of the fire. She closed her eyes and he was everything in her world.

His scent, his touch, his sound. She breathed in and out, and if it wasn't a dream she would never be the same again. He held her close and she let the night take her consciousness...

She came alert suddenly when he lifted her, her senses alive and her body deep in lethargy. He held her in his arms and climbed the stairs, her body naked in his and her hand reaching up to touch his chest. She stared at her own hand against his skin. Then she looked up into the shadows that formed the planes of his face. When he looked down she was trapped and there were no words.

He lowered her to a big bed that swallowed her. She was lying on top of the covers and he come down on to her, drawing a spread over them both and shutting out the world. His room. His bed.

'No words,' he breathed.

'No,' she whispered back. She touched his face. If she spoke now it would be the end. She would say all the words, and he would know secrets beyond the deepest parts of her soul.

His face was hard, and she drew her fingers over the planes and angles and felt his breathing change and touched his shoulder too, and he touched her lips with his fingers, and it was as if she had never known the shape of him before, because she traced him now with her touch and he echoed her motions in a silent Braille that took the night deeper into forever.

No words.

He touched her thigh. She traced the plane of his hard abdomen and his pulse-beat against her fingers. He traced the most sensitive flesh inside her thigh and made her heart stop as he brushed against the heart of her. Her hand closed over his need as she melted into his caress.

Her mouth was hungry on his flesh. The night was heavy with silent caresses. His mouth was on her, his kiss over the trembling of her abdomen, the heart of her need. Silent cries and she tasted his flesh and his passion and needed him and lost herself there. The explosion silent and forever and only breathing and the hard dampness of his flesh as she burrowed against him in the aftermath of the fire and his arms locked her against his body where she ached to be.

The sleep was dreamless. Her heart had been emptied in the silent loving that went before.

She woke alone.

The sun was on her body. She twisted away from it, tangling herself in the fabric that covered her. The heat of the morning sun's rays rested uncomfortably on her back as she burrowed against a down pillow. She buried her face in it and felt her body tremble in the echo of the dream.

Then she opened her eyes, because it was not a dream.

The spread tangled around her arm. It was brown and rust-coloured, earth tones like the blanket under her. She hadn't bothered to climb under the blanket when she went to bed. When she...

She had not slept alone.

She had run into the water in moonlight with Connar watching. He must have thought she was crazy, driven into the water, taunting him, and of course he hadn't followed her. What on earth had she thought she was doing?

She closed her eyes and felt the heat flood over her.
It was his bed, and he'd known exactly what she was
doing when she ran from him on the beach. He'd
known what she hadn't been willing to admit. That
she wanted him. That it didn't matter whether it was
right or wrong or if it ever came to more than his
touch driving her beyond madness.

She needed him.

She needed him desperately, but she hadn't been
able to admit it even to herself. So she'd acted like a
fool, running into the water and backing away when
he recognised what she wanted there in the hallway
afterwards. She'd stood while he stripped her and
dried her and then she'd backed away when he
suggested they go exactly where her behaviour must
have told him she wanted to go.

To his bed. To *this* bed.

Last night had been no dream. All her dreams had
been based on one night seven years ago when he'd
touched her and taught her that even the pain of a
woman's initiation into love could turn into fire. He
had made love to her with skill and passion and he'd
filled her dreams for seven years.

But last night...

She stumbled away from the bed. His bed. How
many other women had been here? Did he drive all
his lovers to madness? She heard a sound and she
shuddered and knew that if it was him she would meet
him as he came into the room and it would happen
again, like a drug in her blood, and she would never
be free of it.

Would he look at her and want her again this
morning? Or would his eyes turn ironic with

knowledge of her helplessness? She couldn't bear it if his eyes were cool and distant. Not now.

She pushed the spread away from her, left it trailing on the floor, and stumbled into his bathroom. She left the door open, hardly knowing what she was doing. Then she turned the water on and stepped into the shower and stood with the wetness streaming over her and her eyes closed in an endless stream of clean cold water, washing his touch away.

As if she could!

When she turned off the water she could see his silhouette through the shower curtain. She pulled it back and he handed her a towel. Silently. She wrapped it around herself and concentrated on folding the edge into a knot so that it wouldn't slip. Anything to avoid looking into his eyes, because she had to know the truth and she was afraid.

'You won't be leaving now,' he said.

Something shattered, and his words threw her into the past. Last night and that night seven years ago. They were part of the same whole. She'd come from Connar's bed vulnerable and needy both times. She'd woken both times with the sun too hot on her. Seven years ago he'd been on the verge of leaving her. Today he meant to keep her, but it felt the same because of what she saw in his face—because of what she *didn't* see.

'You won't be leaving now'.

'Was that your plan all along? To trick me into staying?' She wasn't sure how her words got past the knot in her throat, but she understood completely now.

'I always meant you to stay.' His voice was the sound from her television screen. He was the man who stood to one side and probed for truth. She stared at his chest and concentrated on that voice, concentrated on believing that she might reach out and turn a switch and she would be whole again.

'You warned me,' she said. 'You did warn me. I just didn't realise the methods you were prepared to use to get your way. It's nice that the universe arranges itself for your convenience.' She was grasping for words and throwing them at him. Any words to get her through the pain inside. 'You're good at playing events for your benefit. Tell me, is it for Jess? Or is it because you can't admit you made a mistake when you married me?'

She shook her head, and the wetness that was her freshly shampooed hair slid across her face. 'Aren't you going to answer?' she demanded. 'But you only answer the questions you choose to, don't you?'

'That's the first rule of surviving a hostile interview,' he said. 'Only answer what you choose.' He slid one hand into his pocket and said coldly, 'And you are talking nonsense this morning.'

She supposed it had always been this way. He'd manipulated her when she was a child, but it had always seemed the act of someone who cared. She clenched her left hand tightly enough to dig her fingernails into her palm. The pain helped keep her voice steady.

'I'm leaving,' she said distinctly. 'Tomorrow.'

She heard a gasp from behind Connar.

It was Jess!

Connar turned, and Dixie saw her daughter standing in the doorway. She was dressed in blue shorts and a green T-shirt that clashed terribly with the shorts. Her eyes were wide with betrayal. Dixie felt tears welling up, because every time she looked at Jess she would see Connar's eyes looking back at her. She'd spent seven years pretending that the blue of Jess's eyes was a blue that came only from some accident of genes and chromosomes. Now she would spend a lifetime and not believe it any more than she ever had.

Connar's hand touched his daughter's shoulder. Jess jerked back.

'You said we could stay!' Jess's voice was filled with angry hurt. 'You said we'd . . . When you gave me my cereal this morning you said me and Mommy were staying here.'

'Your mom and I have to talk about it.' He pressed her shoulder. 'Go play with the twins while we talk.'

Jess's chin hardened in a way that reminded Dixie of Connar at his most determined.

'Jess,' Conn said gently, and the air seemed to go out of her. She turned and ran out of the room. A moment later they heard the echo of the outside door slamming downstairs.

'You use everything against me,' she whispered to Connar. 'My daughter. My own . . . my own . . .' She spread her hand helplessly, gesturing towards the tumbled bed visible through the door. 'What do you think I am? Do you think I . . . do you think all I need is . . . ?'

He lifted one hand as if to silence her and she gulped her words, but they wouldn't stop.

'Is that all you think I need? Take me to bed and everything will be your way? I want—I want *love*, damn you!' She shuddered at the force of her words echoing in the small room, at the harshness on his face. 'I won't let you use my body against me...against my will... I won't be seduced into... into——'

He stepped towards her, grasped her chin, and forced her to look at him 'Seduced?' he demanded. 'Do you think I'm blind? You stood there with your clothes wet and clinging to your body, staring at me while you showed everything from the way your breathing changed when I watched you to the way your nipples——'

She struck at him with her fist, but he caught her helpless hand in his.

'Hadn't you better grow up?' he growled. 'You're obsessed with words. You want love? What the hell was it that happened here last night? Do I have to get my lines right for you to listen to what's going on between us?'

She shook her head wildly, pulling against his grip. 'Sex is what's going on! That's all! Only sex! As you said before, "simple lust". Well, I can get that anywhere! I can get it from any man—from Alex or Jake or... Don't imagine you've got some sort of monopoly! Don't imagine you're the only man who can satisfy me! I don't need to go into a prison of your making to get—to get...'

He released her and she stumbled back, and she saw the fury in his eyes. Her heart was pounding and her blood racing, and she wasn't sure what words she'd said. 'I didn't... Connar...'

'I think "laid" is the term you're looking for,' he said crudely. 'And if that's what you want, then go. Get out of my house. Go back to whatever you think is waiting for you in Mexico.' He stared at the hand that had gripped hers as if it belonged to a stranger. 'Get on your plane and get the hell out of my life. Take your luggage and your sketches and your needs with you. Run to Alex or whoever you plan to turn that seductive act on next. Jake, you said? Right, then. Get the hell into bed with your Jake. I hope it chokes you.'

She reached one hand towards him.

'Get out,' he said.

'But . . . Jess?'

He made a weary gesture and turned away from her. She followed him into his bedroom. He went to the window and stood looking out. She stared at him across the width of the tumbled bed where they had loved only hours ago. He turned only his head and looked at her as if she were some particularly distasteful weed. 'Don't try to hide from me this time, Dixie. If you do you'll regret it. I'll make certain of that.'

He'd never hated her before, but she'd screamed until she didn't know for certain what words she'd thrown at him. And now his eyes were filled with cold hatred.

'What will you do if I hide?'

'I'll take her.' His voice was empty, like his eyes. 'If you try to keep my daughter from me I promise I'll take her from you, legally and in every other way, and you won't be able to stop me.'

She turned and walked away. Out of his bedroom. Down the hallway. Into the room where she'd slept until last night. She closed the door and opened the dresser. She took out jeans and underwear and a loose sweatshirt that drowned her shape. She dressed slowly, mechanically. When she was done she went to the cupboard for her suitcase.

She emptied the cupboard first, then the drawers of the bureau. She had spread herself through the drawers as if she intended to stay forever. The first part of her marriage had lasted a day, and she'd run from that. Now six days more, and there was nowhere she could escape. She'd learned that much in seven years. She moved from the dresser to the suitcase and back again, and when she had filled the case there were things left over. She'd forgotten the things in the bathroom off her bedroom, shampoo and hairbrush and make-up—all those odds and ends and they wouldn't fit. As if she couldn't fit back into the place she'd come from.

She leaned back against the dresser and stared through the window, at the blue sky and evergreen trees. She could smell the cedars, and she'd never breathe in that smell when she was back in Sue's guest cottage in Mexico. Back to making pictures and yearning for all the things she'd once dreamed of. Back to watching television, but Connar hadn't been on television much lately and he hadn't really explained why. He hadn't told her what the book was really about or why he was here with a new house instead of dashing away to Africa or Central America.

He'd looked at her as if he hated her, and she would spend her life waiting for him. They would watch for him together, Dixie and her daughter—*their* daughter—waiting and not knowing, and the dreams would be unbearable, because without even trying he had taught her that loving could be more than need, more than passion. That it could consume her.

She would take Jess and Wolf back to Mexico. She would go on being an expatriate living in exile. Jess had earned the privilege of being citizen of two countries, of Mexico by birth and Canada by parentage. But Jess had chosen the home she wanted this morning. Jess didn't want to leave.

Dixie didn't want to leave either.

She was running again, packing as if she could escape Connar, and hadn't seven years taught her there was no escape? Last night he'd asked her why she was running, who she feared—Connar or herself. She stared at the suitcase on her bed and knew how much it would hurt if she lived with Connar, needing more than he could give, reaching for him and touching his passion, drowning in the lovemaking, but knowing he could rise from their bed and walk away without looking back.

But she would never be whole again if she left. She loved him in ways she had never dreamed. She loved him endlessly and helplessly and she knew now that she could not erase that love with an act of will.

Could anything hurt as much as living separately from him? And if she stayed ... was there a chance in the world that he might come to love her? She shivered and knew that he could destroy her if she stayed. If he let her stay after the things she'd just said, the things he'd said.

He might walk away, but she didn't have to accept his decrees. She had her own profession, her own income. She could buy plane tickets. If he put the world between them she could follow. He couldn't really prevent her turning up in whatever part of the world he'd gone to. If she chased after him with Jess at her side he could hardly turn her away.

He'd know, of course. He would know exactly how much she loved him, how deeply she needed him. She couldn't hide her needs when she was chasing him across borders and oceans, couldn't pretend that yesterday's love was dead. He would know his power over her.

She gulped and pushed both hands through her hair. 'Grow up', he'd told her back in Mexico 'Figure out what you want'. But he'd reached for her and she'd drowned in him, and now it might be too late. She'd been screaming at him and throwing threats to meet in court, and what in God's name was she doing? Pushing away the man she'd loved forever, the man who was her soulmate, running from him when he'd asked her to stop running.

Hiding from her own heart. Stupid. Cowardly.

Her eyes were dry. She felt dry everywhere, her eyes and her throat. As if she would never be able to cry again. As if she'd dried up and there were no tears for her. Just emptiness. But she would fight for him, fight to undo whatever damage she'd just done. She would follow him to the end of the earth if she had to, a living reminder that the world didn't end with the eleven o'clock news, that he belonged with her.

* * *

He came into her room silently. He shut the door, shutting himself in with her. She stared at his hand as it released the doorknob and wondered what he was thinking as that door clicked. It was a good thing she hadn't let the tears loose. It was enough that she'd screamed at him. He didn't need to see her tears again.

She reached down and took a sweater back out of the suitcase. She refolded it and put it back. She didn't let herself look at his face, but she could see his legs, his arms and hands. He came to the bed with his arms loose at his sides. He stood there without speaking or moving while time stretched forever. She searched for words and found none she could say.

She turned and walked back to the dresser, opened the top drawer. It was empty. There was a snapshot lying on top of the dresser, the Polaroid she'd taken of Connar walking through the water with Jess perched on his shoulders.

She picked it up, put it down again. She went to the cupboard. The only thing left inside was a jacket that wouldn't fit into the suitcase. She took it off its hanger and turned back towards the bed. Connar was sitting beside the suitcase. His face was empty of everything, his mouth straight and hard. She knew then that it was too late. It would be lawyers and courts and there would be no chance for her to fight for his love.

'Your father made me his executor,' he said.

'I'm not surprised,' she said. She crossed to the suitcase and carefully folded the jacket and put it on top of the other clothes she'd packed. It was summertime, and there wasn't much need for a jacket. She had no idea why she'd brought it.

'He hadn't told me. I only found out after he died. His lawyers contacted me. There's money in trust for you. His insurance money. And some shares.' He named a sum, and she tried to turn it into sense. Enough money for a nest-egg for Jess's education. Enough to run away from a man she would carry in her heart.

For a long time there was only the sound of her breathing and his. She stared at his hands, and they were half folded into fists now. She swallowed and closed the suitcase and snapped the locks. The case was bulging, the jacket too much for it. She felt tired and knew she couldn't fight him. She wanted to reach out, to touch, to beg him to let down the barriers. All the issues between them were churning in her head, but none of them seemed as important as knowing that she loved him again, loved him newly and in a way that could never be sealed into dreams. She wondered how long it would hurt if he wouldn't let her stay, and she thought maybe forever.

He'd offered her the part of himself he was willing to give, and she felt the pain of losing that now. Connar laughing with Jess. Connar looking up and catching her sketching him as he frowned over papers while lounging in a lawn chair. Connar reaching for her as she stood in the water, calling her a fool and crushing her wet body against his.

Connar...

He might leave for the excitement of events on the other side of the world, but he would always return. This was his home, and she could have shared it if she hadn't wanted too much. He'd married her, and he was not a man who would ever forget his vows.

Maybe he didn't love her, but he would make all the
motions as if he did. He would never be unfaithful.
He might leave, but he would return for her. For Jess.

She pushed her hands into the pockets of her jeans
and stared at his hands. 'I'm not going to keep Jess
from you,' she said. 'I wouldn't do that.'

He put his hand flat on the closed suitcase. 'Where
are you going?'

She was packed, and she supposed there was
nothing now but to leave. 'Back to Mexico,' she said.
What would he say if she said she'd changed her
mind? He'd know she was crazy, wildly inconsistent,
but might he let her stay? And if she did stay, was
there any chance in this life that she might find a way
to turn the passion of what had happened last night
into something more? Something that stayed in his
eyes when day came?

He had wanted her to stay, a lifetime ago when she
came out of the shower, before she'd screamed a
bunch of wild nonsense at him and he'd told her to
get the hell out of his life. He'd also said he hoped
she choked on Jake if she made him her lover. That
had to be jealousy, didn't it? Or was it hatred?

'If you give me your banking information I'll
transfer your father's funds to you,' he said. 'And
some from me as well.'

Her head jerked, and she was staring into the
hardness of his face, his eyes more black than blue.
'From you? Why?'

'For Jess.' He made a vague gesture. 'If you want
to buy a house for the two of you. I'll help you with
that. I don't want you renting. I . . .' His voice broke
off abruptly, and she saw the muscle in his jaw jerk.

Her heart was tearing, and he was talking finances. She whispered, 'I don't want money.'

'I owe you for six years' support payments. Any court would give you that.'

'I don't want to go to court!' She felt tears on her face. She saw Connar's hand on the suitcase blurring as she blinked. 'I just want . . .' Oh, damn! She hadn't meant to cry again! She shrugged helplessly and rubbed at her eyes with the back of her hand.

'Dixie?'

She gulped and blinked and knew she would have to beg. If she didn't beg him to love her the words would burn in her forever. She watched his hand form into a fist on the case. He moved it as if he would strike the leather surface.

'Your other things are in the room at the end of the corridor,' he said. 'Are you taking them too?'

CHAPTER TEN

DIXIE shook her head in confusion. Connar was sitting on her bed watching her. His eyes had lost the cold distaste they'd held a moment ago.

'What things are in the room down the hall? I'm not missing anything.' Only her heart, and that had been gone a long time.

'Everything from the apartment in Vancouver.'

Her paintings from art school. The killer whale Connar had admired the day he asked her to marry him. Photographs from her childhood. Images of Connar and Aunt Jessie and the beach here on Thetis Island.

'I thought it was all gone,' she said weakly. If he sent her away she would at least have the pictures of him. She would give him time to get over his anger with her and then she would find him. 'I thought the owner of the building would have sold everything off for unpaid rent.'

'No.' He stood up and walked to her window, and it was only his voice coming back to her. His face was hidden from her. She wanted to tell him to turn around, because she needed every clue to his thoughts and sometimes his eyes told her things his voice kept secret.

'I paid the rent on the apartment for a year,' he said. 'I thought you might go there, so I paid the manager too, bribed him to contact me the instant you showed up. Only of course you didn't.'

She'd been in Mexico having his child. She wondered how badly he'd wanted to find her, and whether any part of his reason had been because he missed her.

'Then I brought everything here,' he said. 'I put it in that room you'd used as a studio at the farmhouse. Then I built this place.' His hand made a gesture, as if pointing towards the room where he'd placed her things. 'The room has good light,' he said. 'It might make a reasonable studio.'

The closed door at the end of the hallway. She'd prowled around downstairs, opened every door. But not up here, because his bedroom was up here and she'd had nightmares of standing dressed in satin and lace in his old bedroom while he stared at her without love.

'A studio?' she whispered. 'You did say a studio?'

'The architect said the lighting would be perfect, but you'd have to check for yourself.' He turned around, and all she could see on his face was weariness. His eyes had gone black.

He'd built this house and he'd put a studio in it. He'd said that for all he knew she could have been dead, but he'd made a place for her to work. She had once told herself that nothing less than Connar's love would suffice, but in a minute she would hold her arms out and ask for whatever he could give her if it wasn't too late.

She wasn't a child any more. She didn't imagine he would stay put on this island. His work was important to him in the same way her art was important to her. It was a part of the Connar she loved—his passionate involvement with the affairs of the world. And although he placed that cool mask over his feelings she knew that it was a passionate involvement—that he was a deeply passionate man. She'd always known that, but she'd had the crazy fantasy that one day all the passion of his soul would be focused on her.

'Conn...are you going back overseas?' He wouldn't kick her out, would he? Not when she had Jess with her. And if she stayed, one day he would come back. 'When the book is written you'll go, won't you?'

'Not if you're here,' he said.

'Maybe Jess and I could...' She gulped. 'I could bring Jess to visit you. When you're overseas. If you're somewhere that's safe. If...' Her fingers curled in on themselves. 'If you didn't mind me coming along and...' She swallowed twice as his words finally penetrated. 'What do you mean—"not if we're here"?'

She saw his fingers release, and his fist became only a hand again. His voice sounded husky. 'I'm not about to go dashing into the path of bullets when I've got a family.' He was staring at his hand, his face harsh and rigid.

'Conn...?'

He cleared his throat, still staring at his hand on the suitcase. 'I'm negotiating with the network about a documentary series. There would be travelling, but not...not as much. I wouldn't be...' He made an impatient gesture with his hand. 'Damn! That doesn't matter.'

'Why, Conn? Because of Jess?' But he'd missed her enough to make a room for her.

His voice was flat, empty. 'Because it's time. I'd have more power over what gets aired in the documentary series.' He smiled bleakly and said, 'You wouldn't believe how much truth ends up on the floor of the editing-room. I want control of that.'

She swallowed twice and said, 'It's a career move.'

'I'm being honest with you.' His voice was harsh. 'I could say it was for you and Jess, but the truth is I started negotiating before I found you, before I knew about Jess. All I can say is . . .' He was staring at the suitcase, and she wondered if their two gazes on the same closed suitcase formed some kind of bond.

'What?' she breathed.

She saw his chest expand with a big gulp of air. 'If I were still into living off foreign news bureaux and chasing wars . . .' He looked at her with bleak eyes. 'If you asked me to give it up, then I imagine I would.' She saw his throat move and no words come out, and then he said grimly, 'There's probably not much you could ask that I wouldn't give you.'

She licked her lips and swallowed before she could say words. 'What are you trying to tell me?'

'Please don't leave.' His words were harsh and his eyes desperate. She'd never imagined Conn desperate. She swallowed and tried to get words.

'Why?' she managed. 'For Jess?'

He'd read Jess stories and carried her on his shoulders, and of course he loved her deeply. But he did care about Dixie too. Maybe it wasn't love, but he *cared*. She should be saying yes and grabbing for whatever he was offering her.

He wanted Jess. He loved Jess. Dixie was Jess's mother, and he might not love her, but he was

desperate enough for his daughter that he would make
a good life for Dixie too, even though she'd made him
hate her only half an hour ago. He would be considerate and caring and he'd just said he would pay
her price—whatever it was.

He pushed at his hair and it promptly curled back
on to his forehead. His face was lined, strained. When
his voice came it matched the tension in his face, as
if he'd lost the will to conceal his emotions. 'I know
I pushed too fast when we got married. And again
last night.' She saw his throat spasm and he growled,
'Damn you! I knew you weren't ready, that despite
the way you...' He slashed an angry line over the
suitcase. 'But what the hell could I do with you in my
arms all soft and...and... Yes, I want you to stay
because of Jess; of course that's part of it.'

'And the rest?' Her voice was a fragile breath.

His hands made fists. 'It's you I've spent the last
seven years aching for. And it's worse now.'

'Worse?' she whispered.

'If I have to beg you, I'll beg you.' He took a deep
breath and his eyes flared. She wondered why she'd
never realised that Connar used words easily for
almost anything, but he seldom spoke of his own
needs. 'Give me a chance,' he said now, and she could
hear pain beneath the harshness. 'Let me show you
that it can work.'

She sat down on the bed beside the suitcase, because she was afraid her legs wouldn't hold her any
more. 'Why did you marry me?'

A muscle jumped along his jaw. His eyes were
black. 'I won't pretend I was in love with you,'
he said.

'It was sex, then? Lust, as you said?' She held her breath.

He ran his hand through his hair roughly. 'You drove me mad that year. Every time I came home . . . I kept having these damned fantasies about you. At Christmas when you were walking around with that bloody law student pawing you——'

'Jason,' she said. He'd been jealous! She felt a smile growing deep inside her.

'I told myself it was insane, that you weren't the sort of girl I'd ever have an affair with.' He unclenched his fists. 'You took things far too seriously for anything less than marriage. And I wasn't interested in chasing any girl who had marriage on her mind. But when I went back to Los Angeles I couldn't get Sonya to her apartment fast enough. When you told me you were going to marry Jason I went to Paris, but I had dreams of tearing him away from you so I could have you for myself.'

She clenched her fingers into a fist.

He smiled wryly. 'Yes,' he said. 'You wanted love . . . Well, I was in heavy lust for you and I spent all those months in Paris doing my best to prove that any woman would do. It didn't have to be you.'

She drew in a painful breath, because it was too easy to visualise Connar with other women. 'When I was just a kid I saw you with Elsie,' she whispered. 'I didn't understand then, but when I did . . . Sometimes I wanted to tear Elsie into very small pieces. I wanted to take her hairspray and——'

'You don't need to.' He sat down beside her, the suitcase once again between them. He touched her fingers, and she turned her hand and gripped his tightly. 'It's years since I've been able to make love to any other woman,' he admitted.

She held her breath, because surely a man didn't feel like that unless it was love? What did it matter what words he used? If he felt that it meant he loved her.

'I tried to tell myself Jason was for you, but when you told me it was over I went through hell to keep myself from coming to you. I told myself you were a trap, and I'd vowed all my life to stay out of traps.'

She wouldn't make demands and she wouldn't let him feel trapped. If it killed her she would keep the door open so that he would never look at her and see a prison.

'When I promised to look after you I thought it wouldn't make any difference.' His fingers tightened on hers. 'You were all the family I had left, and of course I'd do what I could to be sure you were OK. I was rational enough until the funeral. If Jason hadn't been there——'

'Connar, the only reason I thought I loved Jason was because he looked like you.'

His eyes flashed, and her lips parted as their gazes locked. Soon the talking would be over.

'I was raging with jealousy,' he said.

'It didn't show.' He'd seemed cold, almost frightening, because she hadn't been able to touch the feeling in him.

'Believe me,' he growled. 'If you'd scratched me you'd have found pure caveman. When I found you in my room wearing that lacy thing I could hardly see for imagining him touching you, his hands taking that scrap of seductive lace off you and——'

'It never happened.' She put her other hand on his arm and felt the tension of his biceps. His face was deeply lined and his eyes shadowed.

'I know,' he said, and she felt her face flame with the memory of the primitive victory in his eyes when he'd discovered she was a virgin.

'Our marriage . . .' He made a harsh sound. 'I did intend to take you to Paris, but I knew I'd be getting a posting to Africa. I didn't expect it so soon, but you're right. I knew you couldn't go with me when it came.' He released her hand. 'I had the arrogant notion that you would accept that without question, that you would be there waiting for me when I found it convenient to come home.'

'I'm sorry I ran away,' she said softly.

'You were right to go,' he said grimly. 'It wouldn't have worked.'

She stood up and went to the dresser where she'd left her handbag. 'I was afraid,' she whispered. 'I was frightened by how much I loved you.'

'I couldn't have told you I loved you then. That was what you wanted, and I couldn't have said the words.'

'I know,' she said. She took the ring he'd given her on their wedding-day out of the zip pocket inside her handbag. She curled her fingers tightly around it. 'You said I was too hung up on the words.' He'd been right.

'If you have to leave I'll let you leave,' he said. 'But promise me you'll never disappear again.' A spasm of pain crossed his face.

She swallowed, and saw the flash of his eyes, as if he were connected even to the small movement of her throat. 'You said I should grow up,' she whispered.

'You said I should figure out what I want. I do know what I want now.'

'I wanted it to be me.' He looked at the room around them. 'I won't live here if you don't stay. I don't think I could.'

'Connar, I've always been so afraid I'd end up begging you to love me that...that I was afraid to love you.' She trembled and said, 'I'm sorry for what I said there—in your bathroom. I don't know what I said, but I'm sorry.'

His lips twisted, but it wasn't a smile. 'You implied that you could get better sex elsewhere. You mentioned a man named Jake.'

She felt her face burn with shame, because she'd meant to hurt with those words. 'I thought you only wanted Jess,' she whispered. 'I was hurting and...I thought I could be any woman and it wouldn't matter to you.' She put down her purse and searched his eyes, because she wasn't sure of anything. He'd cared about her once, had wanted her as recently as last night. But now... 'I need it to be me you want. Only me.'

'There is no other woman who matters,' he vowed in a deep, shaken voice. 'I promise you that, Dixie. There never will be.'

'I couldn't have left,' she whispered. She crossed the distance between them slowly. He stood up to meet her and cupped her chin with his hand.

'And Jake?' he asked. 'What about Jake?'

Her heart began to beat with a slow, heavy pulse. Her lips curved in a smile as old as Eve. 'I kicked him out when he kissed me. It was your arms I wanted. It's always been only you.'

'Say that again,' he demanded.

She let her eyes linger on his, let her voice caress him the way her lips would when the talking was over. 'I love you,' she said clearly. 'I've always loved you. You're the only lover I've ever wanted, the only man I'll ever love.'

She heard the breath drain out of him, and she held out the wedding-ring. He stared at the gold band lying in her palm, and she felt his hand tremble against her face.

'You said you threw it away.' His voice trembled too.

'I couldn't. I tried to once, but I couldn't do it.' She saw the flash of triumph in his eyes and she whispered, 'I love you.'

'I told myself I would never say those words.'

'Why?'

She saw pain flash across his face. 'I can't remember when my father died, but I remember my mother crying. I remember the sadness in her, the pain. I knew it was because she'd loved him so much, and I vowed no one would ever have that power over me, that I'd live free of that sort of trap.'

He took the ring in his hand and stared into her eyes for an endless moment. 'Be sure,' he said. 'I need you to be sure.'

'Darling,' she whispered, 'I'm absolutely certain.'

She saw his love in his eyes. He touched her face and she felt his hand trembling. 'I was terrified when I found you in my room on our wedding night. You were so perfect. I wanted to bury myself in you, to possess you as completely as a man can possess a woman. Instead, when I reached for you...' He stroked the side of her face, her throat. She heard the deep need in his voice. 'You possessed me,' he whispered. 'And then I lost you.'

'But you found me again,' she whispered. 'Thank God you found me.'

He took her hand with his and slowly he slipped the ring on to her finger. 'Don't take it off again,' he begged. His fingers curled into her hair, and he drew her mouth to his. She felt the warm dizziness and let her body melt against his.

'It was worse after I found you again,' he said raggedly.

She slid her arms up and felt him shudder in response. She opened her eyes halfway and looked up into his face as she began to undo his buttons. 'It sounds like an illness,' she whispered. She was caught in the blue of his eyes, heart beating against his, promises in his eyes, and she shuddered to think she might have walked away from what she could see in his eyes now. 'I love you,' she vowed.

He gathered her against him, and she felt his body harden as she melted into him. 'There's no cure. I don't want a cure. I do love you, my darling girl.'

She trembled with his words, and he covered her lips with his and spoke against her mouth. 'Maybe I've been in love with you forever. I don't know. You're tangled so deeply in my soul that I can't believe in a world that doesn't have you in it. I don't want a world without you. I love you, Dixie.'

'Oh, Connar... I love you,' she whispered, and felt her heart fill in a way that had never come true in dreams. She tangled her fingers in his and whispered, 'I want to give you a ring too. I want my mark on you.'

She felt his smile against her mouth. 'We'll have another ceremony,' he promised. His hand caressed the length of her throat, skimmed over the swelling of her breasts and down to the place where the denim of her jeans was zipped over her abdomen. 'Last night, loving you, deep inside you...' He buried his face in her hair and held her close against him, and his voice was shaken, as if he had no more power to keep the love inside him hidden. 'I prayed I could give you another child, that I could keep you with me and watch a living part of us growing within you, knowing that we'd make a life together with our love.'

She took his kiss deep inside of herself, and when she melted against him he took her down on to the bed and pushed the suitcase aside. They were tangled together on the narrow bed where she'd slept alone when she whispered against his mouth, 'Just in case your prayer wasn't answered last night...' She touched his face and let her fingers trace the hard planes that were so much a part of her heart. 'Do you think we could try again? Because I want your child again... and your love... Connar... please...'

His hands framed her face and he looked deeply into her heart as he answered. Not with words. But with his mouth. His body. His heart.

Forever.

Next Month's Romances

Each month you can choose from a wide variety of romance with Mills & Boon. Below are the new titles to look out for next month, why not ask either Mills & Boon Reader Service or your Newsagent to reserve you a copy of the titles you want to buy – just tick the titles you would like and either post to Reader Service or take it to any Newsagent and ask them to order your books.

Please save me the following titles: Please tick   ✓

Title	Author	
A VERY STYLISH AFFAIR	Emma Darcy	
ELEMENT OF RISK	Robyn Donald	
TO HAVE AND TO HOLD	Sally Wentworth	
BURDEN OF INNOCENCE	Patricia Wilson	
LOVERS NOT FRIENDS	Helen Brooks	
THREADS OF DESTINY	Sara Wood	
INNOCENT DECEIVER	Lilian Peake	
WHISPER OF SCANDAL	Kathryn Ross	
CALYPSO'S ENCHANTMENT	Kate Walker	
SAVING THE DEVIL	Sophie Weston	
BETWEEN TWO LOVES	Rosemary Hammond	
DREAM MAN	Quinn Wilder	
STEP IN THE DARK	Marjorie Lewty	
LOVESTORM	Jennifer Taylor	
DECEPTIVE DESIRE	Sally Carr	
A PASSIONATE DECEIT	Kate Proctor	

If you would like to order these books in addition to your regular subscription from Mills & Boon Reader Service please send £1.90 per title to: Mills & Boon Reader Service, Freepost, P.O. Box 236, Croydon, Surrey, CR9 9EL, quote your Subscriber No:.................................... (if applicable) and complete the name and address details below. Alternatively, these books are available from many local Newsagents including W H Smith, J Menzies, Martins and other paperback stockists from 9 December 1994.

Name:..

Address:...

....Post Code:..........................

To Retailer: If you would like to stock M&B books please contact your regular book/magazine wholesaler for details.

You may be mailed with offers from other reputable companies as a result of this application.
If you would rather not take advantage of these opportunities please tick box.   ☐